THE
STORM

AMANDA
MCKINNEY

Paperback ISBN

978-0-9989599-6-2

eBook ISBN

978-0-9989599-7-9

978-0-9989599-8-6

Credits

Editor: Teri Anne Conrad

ALSO BY AMANDA MCKINNEY

And many more to come...

For Mama, again, and forever and ever.

PROLOGUE

THE WIND SHIFTED, sweeping the black smoke across his face and coating his body like a hot, suffocating blanket. Dean's tired eyes began to water as he took a few steps back and turned away. The blaze from the brush fire heated his back, but he knew it was going to take a hell of a lot more than that to thaw out his insides. Underneath his gloves, his fingers were stiff; his knees, his legs, hell, his whole body was stiff from the cold. Not that he cared much. This was his land, and he intended to do whatever was necessary to take care of all two-hundred acres of it.

As quickly as it had shifted toward him, the wind changed directions again, guiding the smoke away. He inhaled deeply, hoping to clear some of the pollution from his lungs.

He turned back to the fire, the heat stinging his dry face. The flames had increased with the wind, flicking and dancing against the dark sky, where the sun had just set. The horses took notice of the heat and took a few steps back, dipping their heads and fading into the background.

"Well, son, I think it's about time for this."

He turned and grinned at the flask in his father's hand. "Thought you'd never ask."

Dean pulled off his gloves, unscrewed the silver cap and took a deep sip. Whiskey. Good ol' whiskey—a dear friend that never let him down. He welcomed the burn down his throat as he handed the flask back to his father, who promptly took a swig.

He took a deep breath and tipped his head up to look at the sky. The stars were beginning to twinkle and the new moon was just showing its crest.

"We'll let this one burn out and call it a night." His father took another sip.

Dean nodded, gazing at the fire. A moment ticked by as he felt the stare of his father at his back.

"You know, son, it's okay to be upset."

Dean looked down for a split-second then looked back up, saying nothing.

"I'm here to listen if you need to talk."

The fire crackled and hissed in front of him.

"There's nothing to say, Dad. She left me for my best friend, that's about it."

"Your best friend since preschool."

Dean's shoulders tensed.

His father stepped closer and handed him the flask. "Women... women are a mystery that men will never, ever understand. They come and go, each relationship serving its own purpose... although, it might take years to understand what that exact purpose was." He paused and then continued, "And then one day, you're going to meet the one, and the second you see her it's going to be like a dagger piercing through your heart. You'll forget your name, all your pride, and she'll be the only thing that matters to you."

Dean took the flask, sipped and handed it back.

"You'll know it in your gut, son. You'll know when she's the right one."

He swallowed the knot in his throat and nodded. After a minute, he said, "Was that how it was with Mom?"

"Yes, sir. Right down to the dagger in my heart."

He smiled. "It'll be forty-three years tomorrow, right?"

"Yep." His father looked past the fire to the house sitting on the horizon. "I'm the luckiest bastard on earth." He looked back at Dean. "And, not just because of her, you know. Because of you."

Dean looked over, surprised at the sudden outflow of emotions from his usually stoic father.

"The day you were born... my whole life changed. You gave me purpose. And a bond, an unbreakable bond that made me a better man. You've grown up to be one hell of a man and I'm proud of you, son. I couldn't be prouder to be your daddy." His voice cracked and Dean swore he saw the reflection of tears in his father's eyes. "Anyway, I love you, son. I just want to make sure you know, and that's that." He cleared his throat. "Alright, I don't know where the hell that came from. Just... don't let some girl drag you down. Chin up." He slapped Dean on the back, immediately shifting back to the emotionless man that Dean held on a pedestal.

"Thanks, Dad." He smiled, unsure how to react, and took the flask from his father.

"I'm going to go close the back fence. You stay here with the fire."

"You sure you don't want me to come? We can do a quick perimeter check. Together."

His father mounted his horse and settled into the saddle. "You mean, make sure those assholes aren't trespassing again tonight? And stealing our damn horses?"

"Yeah."

"Oh, don't worry about that. I've got ol' trusty with me tonight." He reached underneath his jacket and patted the pistol on his belt.

Dean laughed. "Don't go out in a blaze of glory, Dad."

His father grinned, pulled the horse's bridle and set off. Over his shoulder, he yelled, "Be back in fifteen."

As the outline of his father faded into the darkness, Dean reached into his pocket and pulled out his cell phone. He clicked it on and squinted as the bright light shot like a beam through the darkness.

No call. No text.

Dammit.

Damn *her.*

He turned it off, slid it back into his pocket and was suddenly disgusted with how much he cared about a girl he'd only been dating a handful of months.

His father was right. Women come and go, and he'll know when it's the right one.

He shook his head, embarrassed with himself. He wasn't going to waste another second brooding about some chick who obviously never gave a shit about him anyway. And his buddy? Well that son of a bitch can go to hell for all he cared. Honestly, he didn't know who he was more upset with—his cheating girlfriend or his backstabbing best friend.

He took another swig of whiskey.

Whiskey always helps—wise words from his dad.

Sweat began to moisten the T-shirt under his coat and he took a few steps back. The fire was raging now; it'd be at least a few hours before it burned down. He bent down to pick up a stick when he heard voices in the distance.

Raised voices—shouting.

His head snapped up. A tingle shot up his spine.

His eyes widened as he looked toward the shouts, into the darkness.

Dad.

What the hell?

He tossed the stick and jogged over to his horse and jumped on.

"Come on, Dusty." He pulled the reins when—

Pop!

His heart stopped.

Pop! Pop!

Gunshots.

"Go, Dusty!" He dug his heels into the horse's side and took off like a bullet. His pulse raced as he grabbed the pistol from his belt. The cold air whipped past him as Dusty sliced through the dark night.

He strained to listen, but the night had gone silent. No more shots, no more shouting.

Panic began to bubble up.

He flapped the reins. "Come on, buddy, *go.*"

Dammit, it was dark.

Dark as hell.

Finally, up ahead, he spotted something running

toward him—his father's horse... and his father wasn't on him.

Oh, shit.

Dean slowed Dusty and opened his arms as the horse drew closer.

"Whoa girl, *whoa!*"

The mare bolted past him, spooked by the commotion.

"Fuck."

As Dean neared the back fence, his eyes darted around the landscape. He could barely make out the fence line, and just beyond the posts were thick woods that looked like one black mass in the dark night.

He slowed the horse to a walk.

"Dad?" He cupped his hands around his mouth and yelled, *"Dad?"*

Dread filled him as the seconds ticked on.

"Dad?"

Suddenly, the outline of something laying in the field came into view.

His stomach dropped. *Oh, God, no.*

He jumped off his horse and pushed into a jog. The sounds of the night were replaced by a buzzing in his ears. With each step, his heart pounded harder. His legs, suddenly weightless. The world around him became blurry as the lump began to take shape.

"Dad!"

He dropped to his knees.

"Dad!"

Panic seized him as he carefully flipped over his father's body.

His breath stopped.

His heart stopped.

He looked down at his father's lifeless eyes, and the blood trickling from the bullet hole in the center of his forehead.

Adrenaline flooded his veins, his whole body began to tremble.

No, no. His father wasn't dead. This wasn't happening. He was in a bad dream, a horrible nightmare.

No, his father wasn't dead. His hero couldn't be dead. Heroes don't die, right?

He leaned in. "Okay, Dad, you're going to be okay." Tears streamed down his face. "Okay, Dad? You'll be okay, okay? Don't give up, Dad."

He positioned himself over his father's motionless body and began CPR.

"Dad," he sobbed, "*Come on, Dad.*"

His tears wet his father's face as he pounded on his chest, knowing that it was pointless.

Finally, he stopped and looked down at the body of his father. His hero.

His dad was dead.

His dad had been murdered.

Rage shot like electricity through his veins.

Eyes wild, jaw clenched, he slowly stood and looked toward the dark woods. The ice-cold rage vibrated through his body as he raised his gun and began walking to the fence line.

A mad fury exploded through him, and he released a scream that carried through the wind like a crazed animal as he emptied fifteen rounds into the darkness.

CHAPTER 1

THE SLEET PINGED off of Dean's hat as he stared down at the mangled body in the middle of the road.

A single bullet between his eyes.

The last time he'd seen a hole in a man's forehead was six years ago—and that man was his father.

His gut clenched.

He straightened, tightened the grip on his Glock and looked up the jagged cliff that hugged the narrow two-lane road. Ice was already forming in the deep grooves that stretched up into the pitch-black night.

Then, he looked to his right, down the steep ravine.

Hell of a place to leave a body, especially at twelve-thirty in the damn morning.

The location alone led Dean to believe that the killer wanted the body to be found. That, or the killer was panicked, rushed and careless; and if there was one thing he knew about murderers, it was that carelessness almost always led to an arrest.

He looked down at the man's clothes, which were torn and covered in dirt. Designer, the best he could tell. Not that he would know, really, since he purchased most of his clothes from the outlet stores.

What the hell had been done to this man? And more importantly, why? And why leave the body right in the middle of the road?

He took another look around.

The narrow country road was infamous for its hairpin turns, and tonight it was speckled in black ice. He needed to secure the scene from any late-night travelers. STAT.

He reached for his radio.

"Dispatch, send additional units to my location. I've got a man, deceased, in the middle of the damn road."

Crackle, crackle.

"10-4 Officer Walker... looks like Officer Hayes is close by."

"And get Detective Jameson, too."

"10-4."

"And Miss Heathrow, too."

"10-4."

Dean slid the radio into his belt. The sound of the sleet pelting against the cold asphalt buzzed in his ears as he gazed at the body. His mind switched to analytical as he began the first step in putting together the pieces of the puzzle that led to the man's death.

He reached into his inner coat pocket, pulled out a pair of blue latex gloves and slid them over his stiff fingers. He kneeled down and picked up the victim's hand. On the pale wrist was a broken wristwatch, stopped on eleven-seventeen.

He leaned in and looked closely at the oozing red dot

in the man's forehead. This man was shot point-blank; execution-style.

Dean imagined the murderer; pictured him in his head. More often than not, an execution-style murder was conducted by someone seeking justice, revenge, or by a mercenary, exercising the punishment of the law, the way they saw fit. The killer almost always had an agenda, a want, or a desire to have their voice heard. The victim is under complete control of the killer, and forced to look down the barrel of a gun, knowing they're about to take their last breath.

No mercy.

Cold-blooded murder.

A pair of headlights bounced off the cliff and Dean quickly stood up, hoping it wasn't some drunken asshole on the way home from the bar.

Rookie officer Jasper Hayes's patrol car slowly inched behind Dean's. He left his headlights on and stepped out of the car.

"Hey, Walker." Hayes's silhouette stretched across the road as he crossed the pavement.

"That was quick."

Hayes looked down at the body. "Damn."

"Yeah." Dean glanced over his shoulder. "We need roadblocks and flares set up ASAP. All we need is some drunk heading home from the bar and we'll be joining this guy on the asphalt."

"Pretty sure we don't need to worry about that—I just came from town; damn thing's near shut down. Everyone's hunkered down, staying out of the weather."

"Yep, it's a shit night, and going to get worse." He looked at Hayes, who was motionless, gazing down at the dead body. "Which is why I shouldn't have to repeat myself about those flares."

Hayes's head snapped up. "Sorry, sir. I'll get right on that."

As the rookie officer disappeared back toward his car, headlights shone from the opposite direction. Dean shaded his eyes as the truck rolled to a stop just ahead of the curve. Detective Eric Jameson stepped out and looked less than thrilled to be called out at twelve-thirty in the morning.

Dean grinned, noticing Jameson's hair was matted to the side of his head.

A proud Army veteran, Eric Jameson served on the Berry Springs police force for twelve years before being promoted to detective. Never having been married, Jameson's dark hair, dark eyes, and pension for flashing his badge made him popular with the local ladies. But his commitment to the job only allowed for wild, fleeting relationships. At least, that's what he said.

Over the years, Dean and Jameson gained a mutual respect for each other and had formed a solid working relationship—and a ball-busting friendship.

Jameson slipped on a patch of black ice, but caught himself, then made his way across the road.

"Dammit, Walker, why'd you have to find a body in this damn weather?"

"Someone's got to do the real work while you're at home spooning Sergeant Barkowitz."

"Leave my dog out of this. And how do you know I wasn't tucked in bed with a busty blonde, with a nice tight ass?"

"The dried drool trickling down the side of your face."

Jameson grinned and wiped his face. "Alright, smart-ass." He stepped up to the body, looked down and raised his eyebrows. His relaxed demeanor shifted to serious. "Damn. Someone didn't like him very much."

"My thoughts exactly. Shot execution-style." He glanced up. "And thrown off the cliff."

Jameson looked up, shading his eyes from the glare of the ice. "Or fell off. 'Bout a hundred-foot drop."

"Right onto the road."

"Could've been tossed out of a car, or the back of a truck."

Dean shook his head. "Don't think so, he would've rolled if that was the case, and there's no blood on the pavement around him. Would've had road rash too."

Jameson looked back up at the cliff. "Good point. How the hell did he, or whoever, get up there?"

"There's an old dirt road that hugs the cliff. Danger-ous. Hunters use it occasionally. Can't get to it from here, though, you have to drive halfway around the mountain."

Jameson gazed back down, processing. "What the fuck? Assuming he got killed on the cliff, why toss the body where it's definitely going to be found? And, quickly."

"Maybe whoever did this wanted him to be found, or like I said, he could've fallen. You recognize him?"

"Looks familiar, but can't place him. You?" Jameson began sliding latex gloves over his hands.

"Same here; familiar, but that's it."

"A local, then?"

"Possibly. The broken watch on his wrist stopped at eleven-seventeen."

"So he hit the pavement less than an hour ago."

"Assuming that's what stopped his watch, yeah."

"But that doesn't mean the gunshot is fresh."

Dean crouched down. "Rigor Mortis has set in his face, but not the rest of his body—it's fresh."

Jameson kneeled. "You're right." He lightly padded the man's pockets. "Don't feel a wallet."

"Hey, boys!"

Dean and Jameson turned to see Police Chief David McCord emerging from the darkness.

They stood. "Hey, Chief."

"Heard over the scanner."

Known for his gruff personality and serious lack of people-skills, Chief McCord spent most of his single evenings avoiding both of his ex-wives, and working late at the office, and it wasn't uncommon for him to pop in at crime scenes, just like he was now.

"What we got?"

Dean and Jameson stepped to the side as McCord walked up. He looked down. "*Son of a bitch.*"

"What?"

"That's Clint Novak."

"No shit?"

"No shit." McCord kneeled down, scanning the body.

Dean searched his memory. "I went to school with him, he was a few years younger. Quiet kid. Spoiled as shit, though."

Just then, Officer Hayes walked up. "Flares and cones are up, sir." He glanced at all three of the men, not sure who he was supposed to be addressing.

"'Bout time." Dean turned back toward McCord. "That's Earl Novak's boy, right?"

"Yep. He just moved back to town not that long ago. He inherited his dad's estate after he passed away last year. A few miles down the road, actually."

"Where was he before then?"

"That I don't know. Just got married though, less than a year ago."

Dean shot Jameson a glance.

"Who is she?"

"Some doctor. Mind, not medical. Psychology, psychiatry, some crap like that."

"Where's she from?"

"No idea. Don't know a thing else about her."

"Clint had a sister, right?"

"Yep. Julie, quite a bit younger. Almost ten years, I think."

"And his mom passed a long time ago, right?"

"Right."

Suddenly, in the distance, a gravely, pissed off female voice carried through the wind. "Dammit boys, I slid all over the damn road getting here. It better be good."

They turned to see Jessica Heathrow, the towns' medical examiner treading lightly across the slick asphalt. Dressed in khaki overalls and a thick red coat, she popped a rubber band from her wrist and tied back her red hair.

"Morning, sunshine."

"Fuck you, Jameson."

Dean and Jameson grinned as they watched her pull a pair of latex gloves from her pocket. Known for her ball-busting attitude and vocabulary that could make even the toughest trucker shrink in his seat, Jessica fit right in with Berry Springs PD. She'd earned their respect quickly for

7

her efficiency and keen instinct at a crime scene. She was a workhorse and smart as a whip.

Dean stepped back as she tromped up to the body.

She looked down. "Damn."

"Yeah."

Her eyes narrowed and she cocked her head. "Well, double-damn. That's Clint Novak ain't it?"

McCord nodded and she blew out a breath. "Boy, did I have a crush on him in high school. Kind of a weird kid, though." She kneeled down and lightly turned his head. "Not suicide, at first glance." She pointed to the bullet hole. "The shot is right in the middle of his forehead, would've been a hell of an awkward way to hold the gun... he's fresh, too."

Dean squatted down. "His watch broke at eleven-seventeen."

"What?" She glanced up at the cliff, and her eyes rounded. "Oh, shit. Yeah, he fell from the cliff— could've, I mean."

"Or was pushed."

Jameson bit his lip. "Before or after? Did he fall first and then was shot? Or, vice versa?"

Dean shifted his gaze to Jameson. "Could've been shot after, to make sure the job was done."

McCord glanced at the medical examiner. "Jessica will tell us that after she completes the autopsy."

Blocking out the chatter from the boys, Jessica gazed down at the body. "Hmm..." she leaned in closer. "Bullet didn't go through." She cocked her head. "No bruising on the neck or hands, but his body could tell a different story.

I need to take a full look." She stood. "Okay guys, let's photograph the scene and I'll bag 'em up."

Dean leaned in. "I'll want to look at the slug you pull from his head."

"You always do."

McCord glanced over his shoulder. "Hayes, photograph."

"Yes, sir."

As the rookie began taking pictures of the body, Dean, Jameson and McCord split off, looking for evidence.

The sleet began to pick up as Dean walked past the body, imagining the scenario that ended Clint Novak's life.

Clint was a rich kid born and raised in Berry Springs and was recently married—that's literally all he knew about the guy. Well, that and someone had just shot him between the eyes.

He looked up at the steep cliff.

"Gonna be a hell of a climb in this weather." Jameson walked up behind him.

"You just read my mind." Dean began pulling off his latex gloves. "But it can't wait. This ice'll have everything covered by morning, or by the time it would take to drive to the dirt road around the mountain... which might not even be passable at this point."

"Agreed."

"The cliff slopes about ten yards past your truck. Should be a relatively easy hike up."

"Boo-yah."

He slid on his thick gloves, pointed his flashlight and fell into step with Jameson.

Jameson zipped up his jacket. "Son of a bitch, it's cold. Speaking of, what were you doing out this way?"

"Old man Williams placed a call to dispatch about an hour ago complaining of trespassers."

Jameson rolled his eyes. "How many calls is that this week?"

"Two."

"And his average is?"

"Three a week, lately."

"And we've never found anyone on his land, right?"

"Right."

"How far is his house from here?"

"About six miles down the road, but his land stretches just past the ravine." He cut Jameson a glance. "Which, under the circumstances, makes me wonder if tonight's call wasn't a false alarm. He told Ellen he saw flashlights."

"Flashlights? How many?"

"Didn't specify and she didn't ask."

A moment ticked by, then Jameson said, "Wonder if old man Williams decided he wasn't going to put up with trespassers anymore. Finally snapped and took care of it himself. Shot Clint between the eyes."

"Thought's crossed my mind, too. But what the hell would rich-kid Clint be doing wandering around the mountainside in the middle of the night?" He paused. "Alright, should be a rough path right around here."

Dean shined his light and stepped off the road onto the icy trail. Between the pitch-black night, slick rocks, and tree branches that stretched across the path, it was going to be one hell of a climb.

"Comin' up right behind you."

Dean released a thick cedar branch and smirked as it slapped Jameson in the face, causing him to lose his step and slip.

"Dammit, man! Do that again and you're going to get one of these branches in the ass."

"I don't need to hear about your extracurricular activities, man."

"Your mom sure seems to like it."

Dean grabbed two branches, bent them forward and then popped them back—this time, knocking Jameson off his feet.

"*Dammit!* Alright, alright, that's enough." He grumbled as he pushed to his feet. "*Damn* this damn ice." Jameson paused—to take a breath—and shined his light around. "I don't see signs of anyone passing through here lately."

"Me either. The branches look intact, not bent back."

Dean stepped through the dark brush as if he'd been through it a hundred times, while Jameson's breath became labored as he followed behind him.

"Having some trouble back there?"

"Fuck you."

Dean stepped through the tree line and onto the narrow cliff.

Jameson stepped beside him. "Holy shit, you're not kidding it's dangerous. There's what, five-feet from the road to the drop-off?"

"Yeah, like I said, hunters made it awhile back but it's barely traveled on." He shined his flashlight on the narrow dirt road which was overgrown and barely visible—except for fresh tire tracks.

"Bingo."

"Bingo. You check the tracks, I'll survey the edge."

"You got it."

Dean treaded lightly, careful not to step anywhere he didn't have to. He scanned for footprints as he walked up to the road. After sweeping the light across the woods, he kneeled down and leaned in—not a perfect tire track impression, but definitely something.

Ice pellets pounded his back, a few pesky ones finding their way past his collar and down his neck. He yelled over his shoulder.

"Ice is picking up, we need to get this cast ASAP."

Jameson walked over. "Hayes is bringing up the bag."

"Anything on the cliff?"

"Nope. I'll come out here at first light and check again."

Dean stood. "This looks like the best track."

"Okay, step back, I'll get the pictures."

As Jameson snapped away, Hayes burst through the tree line and jogged up to Dean.

"Bag, and umbrella."

Dean raised his eyebrows. "Nice work." He pushed open the umbrella and held it over the tire track as Jameson took a cast and collected soil.

"Alright, guys, let's head back down."

By the time they got back to the scene, Jessica had already bagged and loaded the body, with McCord's help.

McCord shook the sleet from his hat. "Well boys, looks like we've got a murder to solve." He turned to Dean. "You up for it?"

Confused, Dean drew his eyebrows together. "Sorry,

what?" He looked at Jameson, who was smiling at him, then back at McCord.

"I said, are you up for it? We—Jameson, and I—agree. You've got one hell of an eye, and one hell of an analytical mind, and we think you'd make a hell of a detective. You've worked side-by-side with Jameson on dozens of cases. You know the ropes."

Dean shot a look at Jameson, who was the only detective in Berry Springs.

Jameson nodded. "McCord and I talked about it today, ironically. Right after I told him that I put in a transfer to go back to my hometown, down south. Their detective just quit, and you know," he looked up at the dark sky, "Screw this cold weather."

Shocked, Dean looked back at the chief.

"I want you to take this case; work closely with Jameson. If we see a fit—if you want it, and I think you do well enough on this case—we'll officially promote you after." He cocked an eyebrow. "Well?"

Dean nodded. "Hell yeah, sir."

McCord smiled and slapped him on the back. "Perfect. You can start by visiting Clint Novak's new bride and telling her that she just became a widow."

CHAPTER 2

HEIDI'S EYES SHOT open.

She blinked a few times to clear the blurriness, then turned her head.

She was alone in the bed.

She sat up; her thick, wild, curly brown hair falling over her shoulders. The faint sound of pinging on glass had her looking toward the window—the sleet that the weatherman had warned about must've already started.

She glanced at the clock—one-thirty in the morning.

Why wasn't her husband in bed?

She focused on the dim nightlight in the corner of the room and strained to listen to any sounds in the house. Maybe the faucet in the bathroom, the low hum of the television in the den, footsteps down the hall, but, nothing.

Something in her stomach tickled with nerves—like a faint warning bell.

She looked around the massive master bedroom, past the fireplace and out to the observation deck. It was black as coal outside.

She yanked back the down comforter, the cold air

sweeping over her warm body. She pushed out of bed, slid into her furry slippers and into her white, monogrammed robe—the robe that her husband had given her as a wedding gift; which replaced her fuzzy, paisley print robe, that she secretly preferred.

From the foot of the bed, a dark mass emerged.

She smiled and whispered, "Hey Gus, where's Daddy?"

Her ninety-pound coonhound shook his head, his ears flapping wildly against his head.

"Oh, you don't know? Come on, let's find him, okay?"

She started out of the room, with Gus on her heels, but then turned and grabbed her cell phone, knocking a stack of books and her tortoise-shell reading glasses on the floor. The sound echoed through the silent house.

"Dammit."

She bent down, gathered her things and placed them carefully back on the nightstand. She picked up her cold cup of tea—Clint always got on to her for leaving empty tea cups all over the house—and before leaving the room, she took a moment to glance into the bathroom. The glow from the candle nightlight flickered across the marble floor. The bathroom was spotless, except for the books stacked on the floor against the Jacuzzi bathtub where she had soaked just hours before. Her empty wine glass sat on the vanity and she made a mental note to pick it up first thing in the morning. The two-person shower was dry; both closet doors shut—no husband, or sign of him.

Gus's claws clicked on the shiny floor.

"Come on, buddy," she whispered.

After quietly stepping out of the bedroom, she paused and looked down the hall. No lights. No sounds.

She looked across the balcony where the sleet was sliding down the massive windows that looked out to the back lawn and into the woods. The ice sparkled like diamonds against the dark night. A small smile crossed her lips. She'd always loved winter weather. There was just something about the glistening snow and the twinkling ice that clung to the trees and covered the ground below—there was something magical about it, enchanting.

Gus let out a whimper, intrigued by the late night activity, then sauntered downstairs, no doubt heading for the cookie jar in the kitchen.

She crossed the balcony catwalk and tiptoed down the grand staircase, her silk robe flowing behind her. The silver light from the lamp posts outside streamed in through the windows as she padded across the foyer.

Where the hell was her husband?

She checked the main living room, the kitchen—where Gus was sitting patiently next to the dog cookies—and the den.

No husband.

Did he go out? In this weather?

Wide awake and worried now, she briskly made her way to the garage. She opened the door and shock spread over her face.

His truck was gone.

What the hell?

Where the hell had he gone in this weather?

She pulled her cell phone from her pocket. No missed

calls. No texts. She dialed his cell phone, which he always carried with him. No answer.

She dialed again.

No answer.

She closed the door to the garage and walked back to the kitchen, flicked on a small light and slid the cold cup of tea onto the counter. No, on second thought, she rinsed out the cup and put it in the dishwasher. *Good job, Heidi.*

Gus whimpered, again.

"Alright, boy, *geez.*" She tossed him two cookies, then leaned against the counter, crossing her arms over her chest.

Where is Clint? Why hadn't he awoken her to let her know that he was going out?

Her gaze landed on the window.

She pushed off the counter, walked across the kitchen and slid open the door that led to the back patio.

Gus darted outside, his paws sliding on the wood planks before he took off into the darkness.

Sleet bounced off the deck—the roar of the noise blocking any other sound.

She wrapped her robe tightly and looked around for any sign of him.

Nothing.

Her gaze landed on the woods and a feeling of doom washed over her. A sick feeling. She padded across the patio, into the house and slid the door shut.

She pulled out her phone, again, and opened a new text.

Where are you? I'm worried. Call ASAP.
Send.

Scratch, scratch, scratch.

Her head snapped up. Gus pawed at the door, obviously not happy with the weather.

She walked over, slid open the door. "Too cold out there, huh? Come on."

He bounced inside and shook—slinging ice and mud all over the floor.

"Dammit, Gus," she said under her breath as she grabbed a towel and mopped up the mess.

She stood and looked around the kitchen. She sure as hell wasn't going to be able to go back to sleep until she heard from Clint, so she made a cup of Chamomile tea and began to wander aimlessly down the hall.

Although she'd lived in the house for a few months now, she still found herself getting turned around from time to time.

It was a beautiful home. Any new bride would be lucky to hang up her monogrammed robe in the five-hundred square-foot bathroom. But as much as she tried to feel comfortable being thrown into Clint's luxurious lifestyle, the truth was that she felt like a fish out of water, desperately gasping for air.

Heidi was born and raised in West Virginia, in the heart of the Appalachian Mountains, to a free-spirited, hippie mother, and a father who labeled himself a naturalist. Being an only child, her parents doted after her every move. They were an extremely close-knit family, and although they didn't have many "things" her father made sure she had everything she needed. Her mother was a school counselor, turned stay-at-home mom and her father, the local handyman. Her mother taught her to work with her mind; her father, with her hands.

If Heidi wasn't at school, helping in the family garden or running around the woods, she was curled in a corner reading a book—a habit she had picked up from her mother. Heidi's fashion sense was also influenced by her mother. She wore handmade, long skirts and dresses, braids in her hair, and crystals around her neck to keep her aura in check.

Heidi was born a free spirit, and smart as a whip.

At a young age, she was enrolled in an advanced student program in school, which to her schoolmates, meant she was "weird." As the years went on, she accepted that title proudly and immersed herself in reading and learning, graduating valedictorian of her class, with several college courses already under her belt. Heidi received a scholarship to Princeton University where she studied psychology and worked full-time to help pay the bills. Two years after graduation, she opened the doors to her very own clinic in her hometown.

She had her education and career all lined up, but her dating life was a different story. In high school, Heidi didn't have an overabundance of confidence when it came to the opposite sex. Call it lack of experience, or the curse of the late bloomer, or blame the book that she always had in front of her face. But it wasn't until college that she blossomed beyond an A-cup, her hips and backside became curvier, and she'd started experimenting with hair products and makeup. And suddenly, men were falling all over themselves to date her. It shocked her, to say the least—

suddenly, the "smart, weird girl" turned into the "hot, smart woman."

Over the years, Heidi had accepted her fair share of first dates. Men wined and dined her, sent her flowers, wrote her poems, got jealous if she went out with someone else, and it wasn't long before she became exhausted by the whole process. A process—that's what she consid- ered dating to be. While the male psyche fascinated her, she'd never found one that held her interest for more than a few months. She was much more interested in growing her business—her baby.

According to Heidi's mom, the problem was that Heidi never fully invested herself in any relationship. Sure, she enjoyed dating and getting to know men, but after the date was over, she'd go back to her office or stick her nose in a book, and never think of the guy again. Needless to say, Heidi left a trail of broken hearts longer than the Mississippi. She'd been called too much of a free spirit for her own good, and the truth was that Heidi liked being alone far more than suffering through awkward first dates. She had absolutely no problem being single.

Enter Clink Novak.

Heidi met Clint at an airport as they both waited for their flights. She was on her way home from a convention and he was headed to Canada on a hunting trip with his dad. They chatted for an hour. He was intelligent, mature and cute—overall, a nice package. They exchanged numbers and after multiple trips visiting each other, they officially began dating. It was time, right? It was time to be in a serious relationship... right? She was thirty-years-old, after all.

Six months after that—and much to her surprise—Clint popped the question, promising to relocate to her hometown, where he would open his own dental clinic.

To her and her family's surprise, she said yes.

To this day, she wondered why she'd so spontaneously accepted the proposal of marriage, and the only answer she could come up with was that she felt like it was time... time in her life to settle down, lay roots and start a family. She had her education, her career, and the only thing missing was a family.

After that, her life turned into a whirlwind. She was working twelve hour days at her clinic, planning a wedding... and experiencing her first panic attack. *Attacks.* Looking back, she had no doubt that the attacks were her body sending her warning signals, telling her to stop, breathe and reassess. But she didn't listen; she was young, eager and excited at the prospect of marriage and children.

She and Clint had an extravagant wedding ceremony in Hawaii and three days later, his father died from a massive heart attack, just a few years after his mother had passed.

Instead of moving in with Heidi after their marriage as they'd planned, Clint temporarily moved to Berry Springs to take care of family business and get the massive Novak Estate in order. However, one month dragged to six and eventually, the inevitable happened—Clint asked Heidi to relocate to Berry Springs.

Reluctantly, she said yes. She was a wife of almost seven months, who had yet to live with her husband.

And now, two months later, here she was. No clinic, no friends, living in a Southern mansion, that belonged to her husband, not her.

Nestled deep in the Ozark Mountains, the three-story stone mansion sat in the middle of three-hundred acres that included lush pastures filled with livestock, dense woods, streams and hiking trails. The home and land had been passed down through four generations of Novaks'.

The large house had a castle feel to it, with beautiful hardwood floors and intricate woodwork running through each room. Although Clint's parents had recently done a full renovation, they'd kept the rustic, country charm, but had significantly upgraded. Hello massive Jacuzzi bath, in-home theater and state-of-the-art gym. Oh, and there was the elevator, which Heidi never used because of her aversion to tight spaces. Well, that, and her aversion to laziness.

Her only contribution to the home was her old Volkswagen hatchback, her seven-year-old Coonhound, Gus, her crystals, and hundreds of her books.

Heidi sipped her tea and wandered into the library—her favorite room of the house. It reminded her of an old English library from the 1800s. If she were a little girl, she would play for hours in the room, pretending to be a princess, held captive by a handsome knight, who, over time, would fall madly in love with her.

The faint smell of cigar smoke clung to the air as she turned on a dim light. No matter how many times she reminded her husband that smoking was detrimental to his health, he insisted on continuing the late-night ritual, in the library nonetheless. It made her cringe, and in a weird way, she felt like the smoke was disrespectful to the time-

less literature that lined the shelves, which she so passion-
ately cherished.

She stepped up to one of the many walls filled with
books and slowly trailed her fingers over the leather bind-
ings, when, suddenly, Gus's head snapped up. His ears
perked and the hair on his back stood on ends.

Heidi looked out the window to see a pair of headlights winding up the driveway.

Definitely not Clint's truck.

Gus barreled out of the room, barking fiercely. Her
stomach sank as she looked at the clock—nothing good
comes from a visitor at two in the morning.

She set down her tea, tightly wrapped her robe around
herself and glanced at the gun cabinet across the room
where they kept a loaded pistol. Better safe than sorry. She
quickly padded across the room and grabbed the gun.

The car rolled to a stop in front of the house.

Nerves ran through her body.

Gun in hand, she walked to the front door and flicked
on the porch light.

A police car.

Oh no. No, no, no, no.

Eyes round, heart racing, she peered out the window
and watched the officer unfold his massive body from the
car. He had to be at least six-foot-five.

Shaded by darkness, the man looked down, shielding his face from the sleet as he walked across the stone
driveway. He walked briskly, and with intent. Like a
man on a mission. A mission he wanted to get over as
soon as possible.

As he stepped onto the porch, the light washed over his face.

Her stomach tickled.

He paused and took a second to look around, scanning the porch, surveying the area.

The gun on his hip and the hard look on his face told her that she wasn't going to like this visit. The color of his eyes told her he was one of the most handsome men she'd ever seen in her life.

He had dark, almost black hair, which was wet from the precipitation. His uniform fit snuggly over his chest and wide shoulders—the kind of upper body that only came from hours in the gym. And the kind of upper body that made her want to see the lower half.

She straightened and cleared her throat. *Dammit, get a grip, Heidi.*

She watched him glance up at the house, before squaring his shoulders and pushing the doorbell.

Taking a deep breath, she pulled open the front door.

For a split second, his hard face softened and his eyes widened. If she hadn't been looking, she would have missed it because the lines of his face quickly tightened again.

Growling, Gus ran out the door and the man took a step back, but stood strong and tall, looking down at the frantic, barking dog.

"I'm so sorry." Heidi reached down, grabbed Gus's collar and pulled him inside. "Hush, Gus, *that's enough.*" Gus skulked back, but kept his eyes locked on the massive stranger.

"Dr. Novak?"

She straightened. "Yes."

"I'm Detective Dean Walker, Berry Springs PD."

Dread washed over her as she waited to hear what was next.

"I'm sorry to bother you so late... may I come in for a moment?"

"Yes, of course." She stepped back and opened the door widely. "Please, come in."

He stepped over the threshold, his muscular body filling the foyer. She closed the door and remembered that she was still holding her pistol behind her back—which apparently, wasn't lost on him.

"Ma'am, would you mind handing over the gun?"

"Sorry... I'm not used to late night visitors." Her hand was unsteady as she gave it to him.

"It's good to be prepared." He took the gun, looked it over and slid it on the windowsill behind him.

The chill in the air sent a shiver up her spine. She wrapped her arms around herself and forced the words out. "What brings you here this evening... or this morning I mean?

He looked down for a moment and then into her eyes. The intensity made her heart sink.

"Dr. Novak, I'm sorry to tell you that your husband is deceased."

CHAPTER 3

HER BREATH STOPPED. She opened her mouth to speak, but her words caught.

He continued, "I'm sorry, ma'am."

Gus whimpered, tucked his tail and sat, as if understanding the drama that was unfolding around him.

She blinked, her mind beginning to process the information.

Clint was dead.

The shock on her face was momentary. She pulled herself together, inhaled through her nose, exhaled through her mouth. Her eyes leveled on his. Cool, calm and collected, just like her mother had taught her.

"What happened?"

"We found him a few miles down the road, in the middle of the road."

"*What?* Was it a car accident?"

"I don't believe so, ma'am."

"You found *him, his body* in the middle of the road? Out of his truck?"

"Yes."

"Was he run over?"

"No, ma'am."

"What happened, then? Where was the truck?"

"Unconfirmed at this moment."

She shook her head, trying to make sense of the situation. "So he was just in the middle of the road, deceased?"

"Yes, ma'am."

She stared at him for a minute. "If it wasn't a car accident, then how did my husband end up in the middle of the road?"

The detective shifted and she was surprised to see his confident demeanor fade slightly. "It looks like foul play. Ma'am."

Her eyes bugged. *"What?"*

He nodded.

"You mean... he was murdered?"

"From the initial observation it appears that way, yes."

Tingles of shock shot through her body. "Clint was *murdered*?"

"It appears that way."

The adrenaline began to pump through her veins. "What do you mean, it *appears* that way?"

He hesitated and she knew he was weighing how much he should tell her.

"We're rushing the autopsy; we'll know the specifics in a few days."

She narrowed her eyes—a perfectly canned answer.

She wrapped her arms around herself as the panic and confusion began to muddle her thoughts. "Detective Walker, you've come here to tell me that my husband is dead. Can't you please respect me enough to give me the details surrounding his murder?"

His steady gaze remained locked on hers. In a matter-of-fact tone, he responded, "Dr. Novak, your husband was shot and left in the middle of the road. I found his body at twelve-thirty-eight this morning. Myself, and my team, have canvassed the area and will do so again at first light. Your husband is currently with the medical examiner, where an autopsy is slated to begin immediately. Those are the details that I can tell you right now, I sincerely apologize that I don't have more answers for you at this moment."

Her mouth dropped open in shock.

She couldn't believe it.

Behind her, Gus whimpered, shaking her out of her daze. "Um..." She pulled her hand over her mouth and stared blankly out the window. "I'm sorry, I don't know what to... I'm shocked."

A solid minute slid by and she could feel the burn of his stare on her. Her heart raced as she looked over and met his gaze.

His green eyes softened as he looked back at her.

"Is there anything I can do for you right now?" His voice was low and surprisingly soft.

She shook her head.

He looked past her, around the massive house. "Are you okay here?"

She nodded. "Yes."

"Alright then. I'll—

Pop! Pop!

Glass shattered around them, exploding through the air.

"*Get down!*"

Before she could register what was happening, Dean's

massive body lunged toward her, knocking her to the ground. The breath *whooshed* out of her lungs as she hit the hardwood floor.

Pop! Pop! Pop!

Dean pressed his body against hers, cradling her head with the palm of his hand.

Chest heaving, she turned her head. Both front windows had been shot out, glass was everywhere.

"Gus!"

"Stay *down*." His low voice pressed against her ear.

She held her breath, her heart feeling like it could burst through her chest.

The world went quiet.

Motionless, they breathed together, heavy inhales and heavy exhales. Finally, Dean lifted his head, looked around, and lifted off of her.

She pushed up on her elbows, dazed. "Oh, my God."

Staying low, he lightly grabbed her chin and turned it toward him. "Are you okay?" His eyes darted over her body and he repeated the question. "Are you okay?"

For the first time, it registered that the *pops* were gunshots. She could have been shot. *Shot!* Was she shot? She took a mental inventory of her limbs and looked back at Dean.

"Yes, yes, I'm okay. Where's Gus?"

"I'll find him. Is there anyone else in the house? Kids?"

"No. No."

"Okay, listen," he glanced behind her, then turned back, "Wait for my cover and then get behind the staircase. Stay low, and *do not* leave that spot until you hear from me." He pulled her gun from the windowsill, checked the clip and then loaded one in the chamber. "Take this." He paused. "Do you know how to use it?"

"Yes, of course."

"Good. If anyone comes through that door, you shoot, you understand?"

Heart pounding, she nodded.

"Good." He pulled the Glock from his belt. "On three—

"Wait."

His eyes rounded with impatience. "What?"

"Where are you going?"

"To find whoever the hell did this. Okay, on three. One, two, *three*."

Dean jumped up to a stance, his body shielding hers as she pushed herself up from the floor. Her feet slid on broken glass, the palm of her hands sliced as she caught herself.

Dammit!

She found her footing, scrambled across the foyer, her slippers flying off as she moved. Glass stung the bottom of her feet with each step, and after a few terrifying seconds, she dove behind the staircase.

"Gus."

Curled into in a ball, Gus's body lay tucked underneath the staircase, pressed against the wall. He shook like a leaf.

She crawled to him and whispered, "Are you okay?"

She ran her fingers over his trembling body and when they came away dry, she exhaled. No blood—he wasn't hit.

She leaned against the wall, froze, steadied her breathing and listened for any sounds around her. The house was silent, eerily so.

What the *hell* just happened?

Clint was dead—*murdered*—and someone had just tried to shoot her. Not once, not twice, but five times. *What the hell was going on?*

She closed her eyes and took a few deep breaths to calm her racing heartbeat.

Detective Walker. Where was he? Her stomach dropped realizing that she hadn't even asked if he was okay. Had he been shot? *Oh, please, no.*

She gripped the pistol and peered around the corner. A cold draft swept over her skin as sleet pelted in through the shattered windows. The front door was closed. Her slippers lay haphazardly around the shards of glass that covered the stone foyer.

There was no blood on the floor—he hadn't been shot. *Thank God.*

She looked out the windows into the darkness and imagined the landscape outside, where the shooter could have hidden. Directly in front of the house was a stone driveway, lined with iron lamp posts to light the way. And just beyond a manicured lawn, thick woods. Millions of places to hide.

She exhaled and shook her head. Where would Detective Walker even begin to look?

She nervously stroked Gus's head.

Creak.

A chill shot up her spine. She held her breath, gripped Gus with one hand and her pistol with the other.

Creak.

Someone was in the house. Her heart pounded wildly in her chest.

Do not leave that spot until you hear from me. Dean's words replayed in her head.

Creak.

Whoever it was, they were getting closer. Panic swept over her body and she shot Gus a look, laced with warning, to be quiet. Her skin tingled with fear as she held her breath and tried to fade into the blackness.

The dark silhouette of a figure stretched across the floor in front of her.

She wrapped her finger around the trigger and pointed the gun.

The shadow stepped closer.

She raised her gun.

A second slid by before Dean emerged from the shadows.

She blew out an exhale, lowered her gun and looked up at him. The look in his eyes had her drawing back. He towered over her, his face hard, his eyes narrowed, his jaw clenched. He was absolutely terrifying.

If it weren't for the badge on his hip, she'd think her life was in real danger.

Gus released a low growl.

"Hush, boy, *hush*!"

Dean shot the dog a look before turning to her, his face softening minimally. "You're safe." His gaze darted to the growling ball of fur behind her as he stretched out his hand. "You can come out now."

She clasped his large, callused hand as he pulled her up.

"Did you find them?"

"No. Not yet."

She covered her heart with her hand and took a deep breath.

"Are you okay?"

She nodded, dazed. She looked out the window; her thoughts clouded as she stared blankly.

Gus crept out from the corner, eyeing the stranger that had brought so much drama to the evening.

Dean held out his fist for the dog to sniff. "It's okay, buddy, I'm the good guy."

As if his feet were stuck in clay, Gus slowly stepped toward Dean, sniffed, and turned away.

Dean nodded. "Progress."

She tore her eyes away from the shattered glass and looked at him. "What?"

"The dog… your dog. We've made progress."

She rolled her eyes and clicked her tongue. "Sorry. He wouldn't hurt a fly." She ruffled his ears and was relieved when his tail started to wag.

Dean guided her out from the corner as the sounds of sirens wailed in the distance.

"I called for reinforcements. It's going to be a long night, Dr. Novak. I apologize in advance for all the commotion."

"Please, call me Heidi."

"Heidi." He stared at her for a moment and then reached forward and softly swept his fingers over her hair. "You have glass in your hair."

She shook her head, tiny shards falling to the ground. The sirens drew closer and blue and red lights bounced off the trees outside.

She looked down at her robe. "I guess I need to get some actual clothes on."

Headlights cut through the windows, the sleet glistening in the beams. He glanced outside, then back at her. "Take your time. Just come down when you're ready."

He turned and she grabbed his arm.

"Detective Walker?"

"Dean."

"Dean... thank you."

He paused, his steely eyes narrowed. "We'll find who did this."

She inhaled, nodded. "Come on, Gus."

She felt Dean's gaze on her back as she walked up the staircase with Gus close on her heels.

CHAPTER 4

"AND THEN ONE *day, you're going to meet one, and the second you see her it's going to be like a dagger piercing through your heart.*"

His father's words echoed his head as he stepped outside into the darkness. His veins pumped with adrenaline—not just from the bullets that had just whizzed past his head, but because of the woman he had blocked from those bullets.

Like a dagger piercing through your heart.

He'd lost all sense of everything when she'd opened the door—forgot why he was standing on her doorstep, forgot his own name.

She'd sent a lightning bolt of emotion through him the moment they locked eyes.

She was, without question, the most beautiful woman he'd ever seen in his life.

He tugged at his collar. Despite the freezing temperatures, he was hot as hell.

A gust of wind swept across the porch as he scanned the yard. The sleet was still coming down, and he feared the roads would be impassable by morning, which wasn't going to work because he had a shit-ton of work to do on this mountain at first light.

Although he was only two hours into his first case as detective, he surprised himself at how easily he had stepped into the role. Like a comfortable old shoe. One dead body and another attempted murder were definitely going to make a hell of a case. But he was ready. He was never one to run from a fight. He loved challenges; gravitated toward them. The bigger the challenge, the harder he worked and his gut told him that he was going to face his fair share of obstacles over the next few days.

That's fine; he was ready.

He walked down the steps as Officer Travis Willard, who had just begun his shift, jumped out of his patrol car and jogged across the driveway. Officer Hayes, who looked a little too excited to be at yet another crime scene in under two hours, followed closely behind.

Willard slid a hat over his buzzed, brown hair. "No cars on the side of the road, or anywhere I could see. Fuck me, it's cold."

Born and raised in Berry Springs, Travis Willard had followed in his father's footsteps and joined the Berry Springs PD just over three years ago. Willard knew the sacrifice it took to be in law enforcement and the ins-and-outs of the job. He was hardworking and efficient, but the thing Dean appreciated the most about the officer was that he rarely bitched about anything. Well except the weather.

"Did you check the two hunting spots just off the road?"

"Checked them both, nothing. No cars, tracks or people."

"Pass any?"

"No. McCord called me on the way out. He said he tried to call you, but... you were probably getting shot at. Anyway, he wanted me to remind you that considering both of Clint's parents are dead, Clint's sister will need to be informed, after the wife. He also wants us to keep him updated. I'm kinda surprised he didn't come out."

Dean glanced at his watch. "At two in the morning? Not a shot in hell. He stopped by Clint's body earlier, looked beat."

Willard glanced at the stone mansion before looking back at Dean. "What the hell happened?"

"Got shot at."

"Yeah, I got that..."

"I'd just informed Dr. Novak that her husband had been murdered, and not thirty seconds later, bullets rained down on us." He glanced back at the shattered windows.

"You see the guy?"

"Nope."

"Did she?"

"No."

"Does she have any idea who it could be?"

"Not sure yet."

"Where is she?"

"Upstairs. She'll be down in a bit."

"Is she alone in the house?"

His stomach knotted. It was a big house to be alone in. "Yes."

"Hayes filled me in on her husband. Shot between the eyes?"

"Yep."

"So whoever killed him, obviously had a second bullet intended for his wife."

Dean nodded, pulled a flashlight from his pocket and stepped off the porch. "Appears that way. Hayes, stay here, watch the house. Willard, come with me."

"Yes, sir." Hayes walked to the front door as Willard followed Dean to the driveway.

"There's fresh boot tracks at the tree line down here." Sleet pelted his head and shoulders as he stepped off the driveway onto the lawn. "I followed them into the woods, but they faded in the thick brush."

"Too bad it couldn't have happened a few hours from now. The ground will be covered, perfect for tracks."

"Yeah, I'm assuming the shooter knew that."

Willard nodded. "So what do we know about her?"

She's the most beautiful woman I've ever seen in my life. He cleared his throat. "She's newly-married, a doctor, and just moved here. That's it."

"That's all you know?"

"As of this second, yes." He halted and shined his light on the ground. "Tracks are there."

Willard crouched down. "Yeah, barely. Damn, you got a hell of an eye. You said you didn't see him, right?"

"Right. I took this path based on the clearest shot as I saw it." He glanced toward the house. "The shots came in through the windows, but had to be in between the pillars on the porch. Based on that, the shooter had to be in this vicinity."

Willard nodded. "Don't see any bullet casings."

"Five shots. Unless he took the time to find them and pick them up, they're here. Somewhere. We'll find them."

Willard sat back on his heels and looked at Dean, skeptically. "Dude, you're only assuming he shot from right here. He could have shot from anywhere."

Dean cocked his head. "You afraid of a little work, Willard?"

"No, sir. Just... it's a long shot, man. Literally."

"If the casings are here, we'll find them. End of story."

Willard grinned, with a wicked look in his eye. "Make Hayes look for them. All night."

Hell, no. No way in hell he'd leave something that important to a rookie. "I've got a few other things in mind for him."

"Yeah, me, too—typing reports back at the office."

"You not a fan of Hayes?"

Willard pushed off the ground. "He's alright. Just a little too green for my liking."

"You've only been here a few years longer than him. Give the kid a chance."

Willard shrugged. "Alright, what now?"

"Split up, look for any evidence. Especially the casings. I'm going to do a lap around the house. Meet back at the porch in thirty."

"Yes, sir."

Dean stepped out of the woods and glanced up at the sprawling house.

Damn, the Novak's had some money.

A dim light glowed from the far corner of the second floor and he wondered if that was Heidi's bedroom. His thoughts drifted to her white silk robe and how it swept against her smooth, pale skin. He then began to image that robe sliding off her shoulders and falling to the ground... in front of him.

Dammit, Dean.

He shook the thought out of his head and pressed forward. Hayes was following instructions and pacing the front porch looking for anything Dean might've missed.

He liked the guy. He liked his enthusiasm for the job. Yeah, Hayes was green as shit but that wasn't necessarily a bad thing. Sometimes eager rookies—always out to prove themselves—caught the smallest details that cocky veteran officers passed over. And if this whole detective thing worked out, he'd always welcome a fresh pair of eyes.

"How's it goin'?"

Hayes glanced over his shoulder. "Hey, I heard you say that you saw tracks down by the woods, right?"

"Yeah?"

"Come here a sec."

Dean met him at the edge of the porch.

Hayes squatted down and pointed to a small clump of dirt under the window. "Haven't touched it, but look closely, I swear that's boot tread on it."

Dean shined his flashlight and crouched down. "Son of a bitch, Hayes. I think you're right."

Hayes smiled, pleased with himself. Dean was pleased too. Very pleased.

"Nice work." He sat back on his heels. "But never assume, right? This could be from Mrs. Novak herself, or anyone else who came to visit the house recently. We'll ask her."

"Okay."

"If it does belong to our shooter, then this tells me that he must've been watching the house before the sleet started."

"Right, that's what I was thinking… otherwise, there would have been tracks."

"Exactly."

"Nice work. Go get an evidence bag and bag it up."

Hayes nodded and turned on his heel.

"Hayes?"

He spun around. "Yeah?"

"Don't forget to put on gloves first."

"Yes, sir."

Dean grinned as he stood. He glanced back at the woods, where Willard's flashlight bounced off the trees in the distance, before turning and walking around the house.

Manicured shrubs lined the walls—an excellent place for anyone to hide—and lush trees with mulched bases speckled the yard. In the back of the house was a large stone patio complete with an outdoor kitchen, seating area and fire pit, and beyond that, acres and acres of thickly wooded mountains.

His gaze landed on an ATV parked next to the porch. He cocked an eyebrow and walked up to it. The keys were in the ignition. After taking a glance over each shoulder, he hopped on, started the engine and took off along the edge of the property. The cold wind whipped along his jacket as he surveyed the vast area.

If the gossip was correct, the Novak's owned three hundred acres of the mountain, all the way down to the river.

The river… a good place for someone to come and go without being seen on the main roads. He sped up, changed directions and a few minutes later, he burst through the tree line and onto the riverbank.

The sleet melted into the black water, the smell of moldy river water hung in the cold air. Across the river was a bluff, a light sheen of ice shimmering softly against the brown rocks.

Slowly, he drove along the riverbank, his senses on high alert. The darkness of night hindered his ability to see anything, and considering the weather, he'd be inclined to wait until morning to search the river. But for some reason, his gut was telling him to push on.

He carefully maneuvered around a fallen tree, and slowly rode the curve in the river. He squinted and leaned forward.

Just ahead of him, something—a large mass—sat in the middle of the water. As he drove closer, his headlights reflected off a pair of taillights.

A truck.

He pulled his radio.

"Willard, you copy?"

Crackle, crackle.

"Yep."

"Come down to the river. I think I've found Clint's truck."

Pause. "No shit?"

"No shit. Follow the tree line south then head east, when you hit the river bank, I'm about a half-mile down."

"See you soon."

Ten minutes later, two headlights cut through the dark night.

Willard's truck rolled to a stop behind Dean's ATV and he hopped out. "Where the hell did you get that?"

"On the back patio."

"Damn, dude, that's a Can-Am Outlander... those things are like fifteen-thousand dollars."

"Rides like a Yamaha to me."

Willard rolled his eyes and shifted his gaze to the truck. "You think it's Clint's?"

"Most likely, or, if we're lucky, it's whoever the hell shot at me. Call Hayes, tell him to go ask Heidi what Clint drove."

Willard squinted and leaned forward. "Is the freaking door open?"

"Yep."

"Damn things probably flooded."

"Yep, which means that any traceable evidence is probably long gone."

"Maybe that was on purpose then."

"Maybe."

Willard pulled out his phone and typed a text message to Hayes. He glanced at Dean. "You bring your swimsuit?"

"Thought we'd rock, paper, scissors it."

"Fuck that. Go get Hayes. Make him do it."

"No, he's watching the house."

"Fuck, I'll go watch the house."

Just then, a *ding* on Willard's phone. "Hayes says a new, blue, extended-cab Chevy Silverado."

"That's it, then."

Willard cocked his head. "Why the fuck would Clint be driving around down here, or *in* the river?"

"Only one set of tire tracks, too. Apparently, no one came to pick him up."

Willard nodded.

After a moment, Dean grit his teeth, pulled off his gloves and slid out of his coat.

"You're fucking kidding me, Dean. That water's freezing."

"You've never been skinny dipping in the winter?"

"No, my pecker prefers tepid temperatures."

"Cold water shrinks it smaller than it already is, huh?"

"Seriously, wait 'til morning. We'll get Jameson's wetsuit."

Dean laughed out loud.

"Seriously, Dean."

"Willard, who knows who the fuck will mess with this truck tonight. I want eyes on it now. Speaking of, you got your camera?"

Willard shot a look at Dean.

Dean opened his palm. "I won't get it wet. Promise."

Willard groaned, pulled it from his pocket and handed it to him.

"Thanks." He hesitated, took a deep breath. "Here's goes nothing."

He clenched his jaw and strode into the black, freezing water.

Holy. Shit. It was *COLD*.

"Watch the camera, man."

He raised his middle finger and pressed on, the current pushing against his side. Finally, he reached the truck and shined his flashlight inside—keys in the ignition, an opened Budweiser in the cup holder, sunglasses, pen and pack of gum on the console.

No cell phone, no wallet, visible at least.

He shined the light around the cab and stopped on the splatters of blood across the driver's seat.

CHAPTER 5

ICE CLUNG TO Dean's wet clothes as he slid off the ATV and walked across the driveway.

Willard jumped out of his truck. "You're a walking popsicle."

"You're a son of a bitch."

"If we plan to make it home tonight, we need to get going pretty soon."

Dean glanced up at the sky and noticed that ice was already clinging to the tree branches.

He blew out a breath. "Yeah, I know..."

"We'll get the truck towed out, and sent to be scanned for evidence at first light."

Dean inhaled. He hated leaving the truck, but they'd taken the keys and locked it up. That's got to count for something.

He raised his wrist—almost three-thirty in the damn morning. As much as he hated to do it, he knew that risking his fellow officers' lives wasn't an option, and, the roads were getting slicker by the minute.

"Alright, let's call it a night, for now."

They stepped onto the porch.

Hayes stood by the front door with his arms wrapped around himself. At the first sight of Dean, he quickly dropped his arms and straightened. "Find anything?"

"Yep, Clint's truck, submerged in the river."

Hayes's eyes rounded. "No *shit*?"

"No shit. Blood in the cab."

Hayes looked down at Dean's wet clothes. "Did you…"

Willard nodded. "He took one for the team, rookie. A lesson you'll need to learn."

Dean glanced in the window, then turned to Hayes. "I've got to interview the wife; get as many details as I can before she hits the sack. How do you feel about earning a little bit of overtime? Four hours to be exact?"

Hayes cocked an eyebrow. "What do you have in mind?"

"I'm concerned that whoever tried to kill us, is going to come back to finish the job. I need you to stay parked outside her house for the remainder of the night. Watch for anything. Any movement, anything out of place, anything. Every hour, take a lap around the house. Carry your gun."

Willard chuckled behind Dean as Hayes hesitated for a moment before saying, "Uh, sure, yes, sir."

"Good." He turned to Willard. "Head home, be safe. I'll be in contact with you in the morning."

"You got it." Willard grinned as he glanced at Hayes. "Stay warm, rook."

Dean knocked on the door and over his shoulder said, "Come in, thaw out, but keep your eyes outside."

"Yes, sir."

After another unanswered knock, Dean turned the doorknob and stepped inside.

His eyes locked on her as she descended down the staircase.

Her jaw was set, as if trying her best to be strong and in control. A slightly dazed look reflected behind her beautiful eyes—a look he'd seen many, many times after informing a family of tragedy. Her wild, brown hair was tied in a bun on the top of her head, with loose strands flowing around her face. She wore a faded Bob Dylan T-shirt and distressed jeans that hugged her womanly, curvy hips and flip-flops despite the frigid temperatures.

His stomach tickled.

God, she was beautiful. He wanted to kick himself for thinking it during such a morbid time for her, but he couldn't help it. She was stunning.

There was an understated elegance to her; in her posture, the way she moved, the gentle confidence when she spoke. The way her eyes pierced right through him.

He glanced down and shifted his weight.

Get a grip, Dean.

Tucked under her arms were rolls of plastic and in her hands, a broom and a nail gun. She stepped off the staircase and Dean caught a scent of her shampoo.

She paused, took a deep breath. "I'm sorry I took a minute. I... had to call Clint's sister."

A moment of silence slid by and she shook her head, snapping herself back into the moment. "I'm sorry, you guys must be freezing. Please, come in. I was just about to cover the windows. I've got Gus upstairs so he won't bother anyone." She looked at Hayes, whose mouth gaped open as he gazed at the beautiful woman before him. "We haven't met. I'm Heidi."

"Jasper. Uh, I'm Officer Jasper Hayes."

"Officer Hayes, it's a pleasure to meet you. Thank you for coming out."

She was calm, cool and collected. The only telltale sign of her horrific evening was the flush on her cheeks and neck.

Dean took the plastic from her hands. "We'll get that for you." He took the nail gun and broom.

She frowned. "Are you... wet?"

Despite the ice clinging to his legs, he'd almost forgotten.

"Oh. Yes." He looked down, took a step toward the door. "Sorry."

"Please, don't worry about it. Why are you wet?"

"We think we found your husband's truck in the river." Her eyebrows shot up. "What?"

"We'll tow it out and send it off at first light."

"Why the hell was he down at the river?"

"I was going to ask you the same thing."

She shook her head, bewildered. "I haven't got a clue. Especially in this weather. I have absolutely no idea."

Dammit. "Okay. We'll do a thorough inspection of the vehicle tomorrow."

She nodded and under her breath, she said, "What an absolute nightmare."

Dean's heart broke seeing the pain and confusion in her eyes. He wanted to scoop her up, into his arms, and tell her everything was going to be okay.

"Officer Hayes will stay outside tonight, monitoring the house for the remainder of the evening. He'll walk the perimeter every hour. And, if it's alright, I'd like to have a quick chat with you before I head out."

She glanced at Hayes and a look of pity crossed her face. "No, it's fine, I don't need him to do that. I'll be fine."

"I insist," Hayes said as he puffed out his chest.

"It's settled."

She shook her head and blew out a breath. "Thank you. That... that eases me a bit, thank you."

Hayes smiled from ear to ear and Dean handed him the plastic and nail gun. "Why don't you block the windows for Dr.—"

"Heidi."

"Heidi. Block the windows for Heidi, while we talk for a moment, but take pictures first."

"Yes, sir."

As Hayes turned and carefully walked across the broken glass, Heidi motioned Dean toward the kitchen.

"Can I get you some coffee?" She led the way, flicking on lights as they walked through the house.

Like a magnet, Dean's gaze fell to her backside, which was everything he'd imagined it would be. Perky, round and the perfect size to grab a hold of.

He cleared his throat. "No, thank you."

After tearing his eyes away from her perfect ass, he looked around. The house was stunning, with a rustic old-world charm. In the foyer, a candle-covered chandelier hung high from the ceiling, between massive log beams.

Handcrafted, antique furniture filled each room and he cocked an eyebrow when they passed an elevator.

He glanced at the pictures lining the wall. Pictures of Clint as a child on hunting trips with his dad; extravagant beach vacations; a picture of him behind the wheel of a private jet. Family photos of each of the Novak generations, and more of Clint and his sister as a child. But one thing stood out to Dean—not a single picture of Heidi. Anywhere. Not one of their wedding day, nothing. He made a mental note of this as he stepped into the gigantic kitchen.

Dozens of copper cookware hung from the ceiling above a marble island in the middle of the room. Upscale appliances lined the walls and just beyond the walk-in refrigerator was a comfortable seating area that looked out to the back patio. But without question, Dean's favorite feature was the authentic pizza oven. Damn, what he could do with that. Throw a keg in the fridge and he'd never leave the house.

The only thing that seemed out of place was the string of crystal suncatchers hanging from the window above the sink. Something told him that was Heidi's contribution to the room.

Heidi paused for a moment and looked around, as if she wasn't quite sure what to do with herself.

Dean had seen every reaction imaginable when a family member was told that their loved one was dead. Shock and disbelief were the most common, with unbridled hysteria a close second. Anger and blame third, and somewhere in distant fourth place was strength and composure. Which is what he saw from Heidi. However, he'd never been in a situation where the person who had just found out that her husband was dead, was targeted seconds later. Regardless, she kept a hold of her emotions.

After a moment, she said, "So you have some questions for me?"

"Yes." He stood in the doorway, doing his best to avoid getting mud all over the spotless kitchen, or intrude on her space. "If it's too late, I understand, it's just always best to get some initial questions asked while everything is still fresh."

She nodded. "I'll do whatever I need to do to help, detective."

"Dean."

She smiled slightly and nodded. "Okay." She turned. "It's a little too late... or early I should say, for wine, so I'll make some coffee." She walked over to the silver machine—that looked like a robot—and began busying herself by scooping grounds into what looked like the head. "Okay, shoot the questions, Dean."

He watched her steady hand press the buttons and was almost awestruck with her ability to remain calm and in control under such an intense situation. He knew that inside she must be riddled with nerves, but she didn't show it. Hell, the woman had just been shot at. If he hadn't been there, she would have taken her last breath an hour ago. She'd be dead right now. And he knew that she knew that.

He also knew, without question, that this was one hell of a strong woman. And dammit if his only weakness wasn't a strong, beautiful woman.

"Heidi, do you know who would want to target your husband?"

"You mean, want him dead?"

"Right."

Her hands dropped as the coffee pot began to spit and gurgle.

"No... no, I don't. I'm not aware of anyone he had issues with, at all."

"Think closely. Friends, family? Any recent arguments he might have vented to you about?"

She thought for a moment. "No, I really can't think of anything."

"What did your husband do for a living?"

"He's a..." she looked down. "I guess I should say *was* a dentist."

Dean searched his memory. He didn't remember hearing that Clint had become a dentist, but then again, Dean was older and they hadn't run in the same circles in high school. The day after graduation, Clint left town to go to some big-shot college and Dean had never heard of him again.

"It's my understanding that he, or you two, just moved here?"

Without waiting for the coffee to finish, she poured a cup. "Yes. Well, he's been back for eight months or so, to attend to everything surrounding his father's passing, and I just moved here two months ago."

"Why didn't you come together?"

"I had to close my office first, before moving here."

He noticed a sadness in her eyes as she said it. "Psychology, correct?" He had a fifty-fifty shot between a psychiatrist and psychologist, and based on his short inter-actions with her so far, she seemed like the type of woman whose goal was to help and cure, not medicate. So he went with psychologist.

"Yes."

Boo-yah. "You moved here, to be with him, correct?"

"That's correct. Our plans kind of… took a turn when his dad died."

"What were those plans?"

"He was going to move to my hometown where I had recently opened my practice."

"And where is that?"

"Belle Ridge, West Virginia."

"In the mountains."

She smiled. "Yes."

"I've been to that area. It's beautiful."

"Yes, it is. You should see it in the fall. I was born and raised there. Grew up in a little house right in the middle of the woods."

He smiled. Fall was his favorite time of year, especially in the mountains.

She continued, "Anyway, we got married, and three days later, his dad passed away. He came here to tend to business and… never left. So after months of discussions, I picked up and moved here." She sipped her coffee. "Clint's family has such a legacy here; he wanted to pick up where his dad left off, and lay roots." She laughed a humorless laugh. "To be honest detective, I mean, Dean, it felt like more of an ultimatum."

He watched her for a moment. She held resentment toward the man she'd just committed her life to, for making her leave everything she loved. He wanted to know more.

"That must have been tough."

"Sure."

"How long have you two been married?"

"Just under a year."

"And how much of that time were you actually sleeping in the same house?"

"Two months." She shook her head. "The last two months."

"How long had you dated before getting married?"

"Six months."

So in reality, she barely knew the guy. So why did she take the plunge? He didn't take her for the type of woman to act irrationally.

She sipped her coffee and he saw the glint of tears in her eyes. He glanced at the clock—it was pushing three in the morning and he knew, at this point, she needed to be alone and begin to process the horrific evening.

But he just had one more question.

He took a step forward, and she turned toward him.

"Heidi, do you know anyone who would want to hurt you?"

She paused, something flickered in her eyes, and he caught it. "No, I can't think of anyone. Especially no one that would come for both of us, my husband and me." Her expression glazed over as she glanced out the window.

A minute of silence passed.

"Okay." He waited a beat to see if she would keep talking and when she didn't, he said, "I know you need some time to digest things. Officer Hayes will be outside all night, and he'll be available for anything you might need. I'll be back again tomorrow, at first light." He paused—he was never good at consoling victims, or being empathetic, or saying the right thing, really. So he went with the old cliché. "I'm sorry for your loss."

He shifted his weight to turn and leave, but hesitated—and that hesitation shocked the hell out of him. He didn't want to leave. He didn't want to leave *her*. His feet were like magnets, stuck to the ground. His mind started racing, thinking of any possible way he could stay with her. Any reason at all, but came up short. He knew she would be safe with Hayes on watch until sunrise, but something nagged at him, pulling at him to stay. Was she still in danger? Would the shooter come back to try to finish the job? Maybe, maybe not, but he knew that he couldn't pack her in a bulletproof box and stick her in his pocket to keep her safe. That wasn't his job. His job wasn't to be a bodyguard to the survivor; his job was to find out who the fuck tried to kill that survivor.

And he would. He would go to the ends of the earth to find who tried to kill Heidi Novak.

He reached into his pocket, pulled out a card and handed it to her. "If you think of anything, need anything at all; if you feel scared, anything, give me a call. No matter what time it is."

She looked up at him and a soft smile crossed her lips. "Thank you."

"I'll see you again, in just a few hours."

She smiled. "I'll walk you out."

As they reached the front door, Hayes had just finished nailing the plastic around the window. He turned and smiled, obviously pleased with his work.

"Thank you so much, Officer Hayes. I just put some coffee on; would you like a cup?"

"Yes, ma'am."

"It's in the kitchen. Just help yourself."

"Thank you."

As Hayes disappeared across the house, Heidi opened the front door and turned to Dean. "Thank you, again, for everything."

He lingered. "Are you sure you're okay?"

"Yes, I'll be fine."

"Okay." He stared at her for a moment. "Alright, I'll see you in the morning."

"Good night, Dean."

He felt her eyes on him as he turned and walked to his car.

CHAPTER 6

AS HAYES WALKED down the hall, he marveled at the old house. Correction, old *mansion*. He preferred a little log cabin any day of the week, but he could sure see himself living in this castle. Each room led to another, and another. And each room was bigger than the next.

The places he could've hidden playing hide-and-seek if he had grown up in this house.

He stepped into the kitchen and stopped in his tracks when he saw a young blonde—super sexy, in his opinion—wide-eyed, and gazing out the window with worry written all over her face.

He cocked his head. She was dressed... oddly, to say the least. She wore plaid pajama bottoms, furry boots that look ten sizes too big and a hooded sweatshirt underneath a camo winter jacket. Her blonde hair was pulled back; messy and sticking out from all angles of her head.

He hadn't expected to see anyone else beside Heidi in the house, let alone this little damsel in distress. Were there hot chicks in every room of this place?

As if feeling the presence of someone behind her, she

looked over her shoulder and gasped when she saw him. She pushed herself away from the counter and took a few steps toward him.

"Officer..." Her voice was quick, and panicked. "Is everything okay?"

He puffed out his chest and deepened his voice. Women love authority, after all.

"Yes, ma'am. Everything's okay now. I've got things under control. I don't believe we've met..."

She blew out a breath of relief, distracted. "Thank *God* everyone's okay. I... I thought I heard shots, and when I saw the police lights, I freaked out."

He crossed the room. "I'm sorry, your name is?"

"Oh, I'm so sorry. Eve. My name is Eve. I'm the Novak's personal chef and maid. Well, less of a maid since Heidi moved in. She's so sweet; cleans and everything."

He stretched out his hand. "Officer Hayes, BSPD."

She smiled, her eyes sparkling. "Pleasure to meet you." A line of worry ran between her eyebrows. "What happened? Is Heidi okay?"

"Yes, she's in the foyer, speaking with the detective right now."

She looked past him. "Did I hear gunshots? Were they gunshots?"

He shifted his weight. He wasn't quite sure how much Dean wanted him to share, but gunshots were gunshots, it was hard to mistake that.

"Yes, ma'am."

She gasped. "Oh, dear. But Heidi's okay, you said?"

"Yes, ma'am."

"Okay, as long as everyone's okay. My God, how scary. What... who was shooting?"

"Unconfirmed at this time."

"Hunters, maybe?"

"We're looking into that."

"Did Heidi or Clint call the cops? Did someone shoot at the house?"

He paused. "Heidi called. And, yes, shots were fired at the front windows. Whether it was on purpose, or an accident, we don't know."

"Oh, my God. How terrifying."

"Were you in the house?"

"No, I live across the field. I heard gunshots, but thought maybe I was crazy. But then I saw all the commotion. I knew Heidi would call if she needed me, but I was worried—so I jumped on my ATV and came over.

Ah, hence the attire.

"Did you see anyone?"

"No, no, I don't think so, but I wasn't looking, to be honest."

"Any cars?"

"No."

"Hear any cars on the dirt road?"

"No, I don't think so, but I wasn't really listening for anything."

"How long ago did you hear the gunshots?"

"Um, an hour ago, maybe longer?"

He cocked his head. "And you didn't come over immediately?"

"No, like I said, I thought maybe I was crazy, just hearing things, but when I saw the police lights, I knew something had happened. So I waited by the phone, but then couldn't take it—I was too worried.

"Okay, were you with anyone when you heard the shots?"

She blinked, paused. "No, I was just on my couch, watching television, with a glass of wine. I stay up late."

"Sounds like an eventful evening."

She shifted nervously. "I'm sorry. Would you like some coffee? I see Heidi started a pot."

"Yes, ma'am, please."

He glanced down at her backside as she turned, but dammit, it was covered with that enormous, oversized camo coat. Well, he could imagine at least—and he imagined that it was a tight, perfect little ass.

"Would you like cream or sugar?"

I'd like a little of your sugar. "Both, please."

"Okay." She stirred in the condiments and handed him a mug with kittens printed on the front.

He sipped, and burned the shit out of his tongue. He winced, but quickly regained his composure before she noticed. "Thank you."

"Yes, sir."

Sir. Sir sounded good, *real good.* Yes, he was the authority here.

He eyed her over the rim as he took another sip—a tiny sip. There was no way in hell that he was much older than she was. He guessed she was, twenty-one, twenty-two maybe? Regardless, he was older and carried a badge, and all women liked an older man in a uniform, right?

Eve started across the room. "I need to go talk to Heidi, make sure she's okay."

"She's speaking with the detective now. Please give her a minute."

She stopped. "Oh. Okay."

She seemed nervous, unsure what to do with an officer standing in her kitchen. So he did his best to ease her.

He casually leaned against the counter. "How long have lived you here?"

Before she could answer, Heidi walked into the kitchen and her eyes rounded when she saw Eve.

"Eve, what are you doing here?"

"Oh, Heidi, are you okay?"

"Yes, I'm fine. Well," she glanced at Hayes. "Have you told her?"

He shook his head. "No, ma'am..." He set his coffee on the table. "I'll give you two some privacy. I'm going to do a perimeter check. Has Dean left already?"

Heidi nodded and turned back toward Eve, her face awash with sadness.

"Eve, honey, let's go to the den. We need to talk."

CHAPTER 7

HE BLEW OUT a breath, peeling his fingers off the steering wheel before turning off the engine.

What a hell of a drive home.

He'd driven on ice more times than he could count, but not usually at three in the morning—after being shot at.

Even after picking up his four-wheel drive at the station, he'd still slid out of the parking lot. If McCord deemed him worthy to officially promote him to full-time detective, he'd get his own unmarked car, but not today.

He grabbed his cellphone, gun and pushed out of the door. The sleet was just beginning to let up, which was a necessity if he was going to make it back out to the Novak Estate in the morning.

And hell on earth couldn't stop that.

He walked up the stone walkway to his porch and pulled out his keys.

A black flash darted out from behind the rocking chair, taking about five years off his life.

"*Dammit*, Diablo."

Diablo—the Spanish word for Devil—was the name

he had lovingly given to the stray, feral cat that refused to leave his house.

Every week, the black cat would work its way into Dean's trash can, dragging half the contents through the yard. Dean had purchased three different trash cans with lids, but Diablo always found a way. On nights that the devil was feeling particularly sinful, Dean would wake up to paw prints all over his freshly washed truck. That really pissed him off. He didn't know if Diablo was male or female, but he assumed a male because no woman on earth was as cold-hearted as that damn cat.

After sending another menacing glare in the devil cat's direction, he unlocked the front door and pushed it open. It was dark, and ice-cold. A sour scent hung in the air reminding him that he needed to take out the trash, immediately. Diablo would have a hell of a time with whatever was making that smell.

He flicked on the lights, pulled off his jacket and hung it on the wall-rack that his mother had gotten him.

He took a deep breath and an ounce of tension released from his shoulders, just being home.

Nestled deep in the town's largest mountain, Summit Mountain, Dean lived in a small, two bedroom, two bathroom rock and log cabin. He'd bought the house years ago for two reasons—one, he could afford it, and two, its property line backed up to his parent's two-hundred-acre property. The property he would inherit someday.

The year he moved in, he'd spent every spare second renovating it, making it just the way he wanted. He'd put cherry red hardwood floors in every room; a new stone fireplace in the living room; new roof; new porch and had completely remodeled the kitchen and bathrooms. He'd meticulously picked out every color, material and fabric to reflect the nature outside. Native American rugs ran through the house; leather and dark plaid furniture decorated the rooms, and family pictures lined the walls. His bedroom was centered around a four-poster king-sized bed overlooking the woods. He didn't believe in televisions in the bedroom—an opinion he'd picked up from his father. His bathroom—the most important room in the house—had a two-person stone shower, a separate toilet, of course, and an enormous Jacuzzi tub that sat in the corner against windows that looked out into the woods. Copper sinks completed a his-and-her vanity. Although there was no "her" yet.

The house was definitely a bachelor pad, and that was just fine with him.

Born and raised in Berry Springs, Dean grew up an only child to his saint of a mother, Nancy, or Nance, a lifelong school teacher. His father, Chuck, his hero, had been a farmer since the day he took his first steps.

Like his dad, Dean grew up working on their ranch every second that he wasn't in school. His father taught him how to take care of the land—raise cattle, tend to the horses, burn pastures, mend fences, haul hay, and harvest crops. The work was endless. His father also taught him how to shoot guns, fish, and hunt. Dean lived and breathed the outdoors.

He was a true country boy, through and through.

And one hell of a football player. A muscular six-foot four-inches tall, Dean was the all-star quarterback of Berry Springs High School. After one particularly successful game, Dean was approached by recruiters from several universities, and was eventually offered a full ride to two separate schools. True to form, his mother promptly called a family meeting, to discuss all the paths that his future could take, and the Walker legacy.

He'll never forget that day. They gathered around the kitchen table, in their humble, three bedroom, two bathroom ranch house. He was still sweaty from his last workout, and his hands were wrapped around an ice-cold Gatorade. His mother stood and nervously began cleaning the dishes as his father started the conversation by saying: "*Son, it's time you learned a few things about your heritage.*" For the next hour, his father told him stories he'd never heard before about his grandfather and great-grandfather. He talked to him about hard work, perseverance, and responsibility.

Dean listened with intent, as if he knew that the evening was going to change his life. Finally, his father stood, got a pen and paper, and wrote *Walker Assets* on the top. It was then that Dean learned that the Walker Estate had over one-million dollars in liquid assets, and that the family had a responsibility to take care of everything that his grandfather and great-grandfather had worked for.

But the big news came when his father told him about the two-and-a-half million dollars they had sitting in a savings account.

He was stunned, *shocked*. Never, in his wildest dreams, had he imagined that they had money. His father was the most frugal man he'd ever met, and his mom, the most self-less woman on the planet. No designer handbags or clothes for her, no sir.

Growing up, his parents had made him pay for anything that wasn't a "necessity"—as they would call it—out of his own savings account, which he filled with his weekly allowance. The day he turned sixteen, his father pushed him to get a job bagging groceries at the local grocery store, which was in addition to his daily chores on the ranch. His parents had even made him pay for his first truck, which he worked his ass off to do.

His father explained that the money had been passed down through the Walker generations; through years of hard work. He explained that the moment he and Dean's mother found out that she was pregnant, they promised each other to raise a hardworking, Southern gentleman who never felt a sense of entitlement.

Well, they definitely succeeded there.

By the end of the conversation, Dean understood why his father had kept the money a secret, and had more respect for his parents than ever. For the first time, he looked at them as *people*, not just his parents, and with complete admiration.

That single conversation was Dean's first step toward becoming a man. He'd realized the conversation wasn't about the money; it was about accepting the responsibility to take care of what was theirs—his. That was the lesson his father had taught him that evening.

To *always* take care of what was *his*.

A few months later, Dean set off to play college football and graduated with a major in Agriculture and a minor in Business. The day after graduation, he moved back to Berry Springs to pick up where he left off, and help his father take care of the land, and what was his.

Dean worked hard every day, seven days a week, from

dawn until dusk maintaining the massive property and all of the livestock. Because of Dean's help, his father was able to focus more on the crops, which was his true passion.

Dean's work ethic and commitment to his land didn't leave much time for other things in his life, especially women. Getting women was never an issue for Dean. His tall, muscular body, athleticism, and boyish good looks made him legendary in Berry Springs *and* in the surrounding towns. But Dean was always more interested in having beers with the boys at Frank's Bar, than courting a woman. Sure, he dated and had plenty of relationships, but the majority of those romantic entanglements were short, to say the least.

The one girl that had actually held his interest for more than a few weeks left him for his best friend, leaving Dean emotional for the first time over a failed relationship.

But that was okay—he learned quickly that women come and go and the world keeps spinning... for better, or for worse.

And the worse, was on its way.

The long days working the ranch ticked on in comfortable routine, until the day that changed his life forever— the day his father was shot in the head while confronting trespassers in the middle of the night.

They say that everyone has at least three experiences in their life that significantly changes the course of their future. That was Dean's. Four months after his father was murdered, Dean quit working full-time on the ranch and joined the police force, to take care of what was his, and to serve and protect the citizens of Berry Springs.

They'd never found the person who did it. The only

piece of evidence was the bullet casing that Dean had found himself, on the ground, the night of the murder. And ever since that day, Dean had compared that casing to the barrel markings on every single murder weapon that was confiscated by Berry Springs PD, in hopes of finding a match.

Six years, and no luck.

Dean walked to the kitchen and glanced at the clock. It was almost four in the morning, but thanks to the adrenaline still lingering in his body, he was wide awake, and wired.

He pulled open the fridge and grabbed a beer. He popped the top, took a swig and leaned against the counter.

He'd seen more than a few dead bodies since joining the police force, but something about tonight made him extra edgy. It wasn't just seeing the finality of death in Clint Novak's eyes as they stared lifelessly up at the black sky. It wasn't just the fact that he and Clint had gone to school together decades earlier. It wasn't just the fact that there was another senseless murder in Berry Springs. No, there was something else about this one that made his stomach clench.

He slowly sipped his beer as the vision of Heidi Novak crept into his head. Her face, her cute freckles and those eyes that seemed to paralyze him. And, *God,* those lips and that body. His intense physical attraction to her was only exceeded by the number of questions he had about her. Although she was as beautiful as a princess, she stuck out like a sore thumb in that old stone castle. She seemed awkward in her surroundings, uncomfortable, as if she knew she didn't quite fit in. But she hid it, and hid it well. Just like she'd tucked away the shock after learning her husband had been murdered. Just like she'd tucked away the adrenaline that pumped through her body after being shot at in her foyer. But he could see it. For some reason, he could see right through her, like he'd known her for years.

He didn't really remember Clint from high school, but one thing that he did remember was that he was a spoiled brat. From the outside looking in, Clint and Heidi didn't fit. Heidi carried a quiet, understated confidence, with a soft kindness to her. Underneath all that armor, of course.

Underneath those tight-fitting jeans.

He shook his head and tried to focus on the murder and not on Heidi's delectable ass. Sure, Clint was an entitled, rich-kid prick, but why would someone kill him? Especially execution style? Finding Clint's truck in the river puzzled the shit out of him. Why was his car left abandoned in an icy river, and his body found more than two miles down the road? The door being left open alluded to two scenarios—one, Clint was in a hell of a hurry to get out of his truck, or two, the killer wanted to wash away evidence.

What was Clint doing down at the river in the first place? Meeting someone? Someone who led him to his death?

But more importantly than all those questions swirling around in his head; why go after his wife, too?

It had to be about money, right? Clint's family had a lot of it, and everyone knew it.

Dean wrinkled his nose in deep thought. Or, an affair, maybe? A crazed, jealous mistress kills the man who swore he'd leave his family for her, but never did, and then goes after the woman that she could never live up to.

It was possible.

He shook his head, feeling the twinge of a headache brewing; took another sip and kicked off his boots, slinging mud and ice all over the stone floor. He wiped up some of the mess with his wet sock and kicked the shoes in the corner. Outside, the ice pinged against the window, reminding him that he needed to get a fire going if he was going to tough out another night without using the heater. Frugality, that's what his father had taught him. And besides, there was something about the smell of burning wood that reminded him of growing up. Warm, happy memories.

He walked down the hall, into the living room and kneeled down in front of the fireplace. After a few minutes, the fire was roaring and the faint smell of smoke drifted through the house. He grabbed his beer and sank into the couch to clear his mind for a minute, before taking a shower and attempting to get some shut-eye.

The house was silent except for the crackling and popping of the burning wood as he stared blankly into the fire.

After a moment, he finally let himself address the thought that he'd been pushing away all night. The thought that had been gnawing at him since he looked down at Clint Novak's mangled body.

The bullet to the head.

The single bullet hole in the middle of his forehead.

Just like his dad.

His chest squeezed as the memories of that night began to flood him. The night that changed his life, *and him*, forever.

He glanced up at the mantel, at a faded picture of him and his father on their first fishing trip. He was five years old.

Damn, he missed him.

Damn the son of a bitch that killed him and still walked free.

If Dean's father had taught him anything, it was to never give up, and he didn't intend to. Not until he put a bullet between the eyes of the man who murdered his father.

CHAPTER 8

DEAN'S EYES DRIFTED open to darkness. In a daze, he rolled over and glanced at the clock—six in the morning. He didn't know which was more shocking—the fact that he'd woken up before his alarm clock, or the fact that he'd woken up before his alarm clock after only getting two hours of sleep.

But that was okay, he was good on little to no sleep. Blame it on late nights and early mornings on the ranch.

He blinked the sleepiness from his eyes. He'd barely slept during the two hours. He'd kept waking up, thinking about the murder… and Heidi. He'd even checked his phone more than ten times to make sure he didn't miss a call or text from her, or Hayes.

He flung off the covers and tensed when the frigid air swept over his warm skin. Dammit, it was cold.

He pushed himself out of bed and looked out the window. The dim glow of dawn sparkled off the ice that coated the trees and the ground below. The woods looked like a magical fairyland. Like something he'd seen on some Disney commercial.

It was beautiful, yet haunting.

In nothing but boxer shorts, he padded to the kitchen to start the coffee. He glanced out the front window at his ice-covered truck and groaned thinking of how many accidents would be called into the station today. No matter how many warnings they issued, it was guaranteed that at least a third of the town would venture out in the weather; to get groceries, go to work, or, in a surprising amount of cases, get booze.

As he scooped the grounds in the maker, his mind raced with all the things he needed to do. At the top of his list was finding out more about Clint and Heidi Novak.

And he knew exactly where to start his investigating.

After a quick shower and a slick drive, Dean slid into a narrow spot between two jacked up dually's and thanked the good Lord above when the truck stopped before hitting the curb. He pressed the emergency brake and checked his phone one more time before turning off the engine.

On the way into town, he'd called Hayes to get an update on his overnight watch. As suspected, no activity other than Heidi and Eve bringing him fresh coffee, freshly baked banana bread, extra blankets and pillows throughout the night. To Dean's surprise, Hayes actually sounded alert and upbeat, and he guessed it had something to do with the women who had been tending to him all evening.

Dean unfolded himself from the cab of his truck and pushed through the front door of the diner. The smell of pancakes, bacon, and sweet maple syrup perfumed the air.

Heaven.

In the middle of town square, Donny's Diner served as the central hub of all things Berry Springs. With its bright red booths, blue and white checkered curtains, and rusty juke box that constantly played classic country music, the diner was as Southern as the cooking. Three things could always be counted on at Donny's—fresh coffee, delicious, greasy Southern food, and endless gossip—which was exactly what Dean counted on today.

"Howdy there, Dean!"

"Hey, Mrs. Booth," Dean replied, while wiping his boots on the welcome mat.

"Slick as a duck's back out there, ain't it?"

"Sure is. You make it in okay?"

"Of course. I just live around the block." She wiped her hands on her apron. "The boys joinin' you?"

"No ma'am, just me this morning."

"Your booth is free; take a seat, I'll be right there."

Dean slid into the back corner booth where he and the boys always gathered for breakfast, to discuss open investigations and swap stories about whatever chaos they'd been called to that day.

Donny's Diner opened at five in the morning, seven days a week and had a line out the door until about ten, then it started all over again for the lunch crowd. But thanks to the slick roads outside, it wasn't nearly as busy as usual for six forty-five in the morning. Only two lone cowboys at the bar, and Mr. and Mrs. Pierson, married sixty years, who came in every morning to solve the daily crossword puzzle while they ate breakfast together, in silence.

He watched Mrs. Booth address all four of her customers by their first names, like she always did. Born and raised in Berry Springs, Mrs. Booth was just as much a staple in town as the diner. With long, gray hair that was always knotted on her head with a yellow number two pencil, she'd worked at Donny's as long as Dean could remember. Literally, since he was a little boy. She knew everyone in town, their parents, and their grandparents, and *all* of their business. Mrs. Booth was a walking box of gossip, with no lid.

She was a detective's best friend.

"You're here earlier than usual." She set an empty cup on the table and filled it with steaming hot coffee.

"Just getting a jump on the day, Mrs. Booth."

She narrowed her eyes and leaned in. "Wouldn't have anything to do with that body found on County Road 43, would it?"

Dean cocked his eyebrow. "And why do you think there was a body found on County Road 43, Mrs. Booth?"

She smiled, pleased with herself. "Daughter-in-law works dispatch, you know that."

Yes, he did know that, and he also knew that Chief McCord recently had a talk with Mrs. Booth's daughter-in-law, Ellen, about confidentiality, and the repercussions of leaking information. But it looked like Ellen was just as much a gossip as her mother-in-law.

"You know Ellen isn't supposed to be talking about that kind of stuff." He shook a sugar packet, ripped off the top and stirred it into his coffee.

"Oh, now, she only told me and, well, I'm family. No secrets." She winked, "And don't worry, I ain't told anyone."

He slid her the side-eye and grinned. "It is early."

She grinned. "You know me too well, son." She straightened, gazing at the ceiling. "Gosh, I remember waitin' on you and your daddy when you were just, oh, four or five years old, probably."

He smiled and looked down.

"Such a wonderful man, he was. So," she lowered her voice, "I hear the guy was shot between the eyes, that true?"

At least Clint's name hadn't been leaked yet.

"You know I can't get into that."

She continued, obviously knowing the information already. "What a terrible, terrible, thing. I mean, who would do that to a man... to anyone. And, here in Berry Springs?" She blew out an exhale. "Makes me want to add another set of locks to my doors... and oil up my shotgun."

Dean grit his teeth. He hated hearing fear in Mrs. Booth's voice, or anyone's in Berry Springs, because it was his job to protect them. Everyone in this town was supposed to feel safe, at all times.

He thought of Heidi and his stomach dropped.

"We'll find who did it, Mrs. Booth." His steely eyes locked on hers. "I can promise you that."

She slowly nodded, her face drawn with concern. "I know you will, dear."

"On that note, I'll take a Western omelet with wheat toast, please, ma'am."

She smiled, happy to change the conversation. "You got it."

Dean watched Mrs. Booth walk away and contemplated how he was going to pull the information he needed from her without spilling Clint Novak's name. His opportunity came moments later when she delivered a basket of warm biscuits, with homemade butter and jelly.

"Thank you."

"You're welcome, dear. Any accidents so far?"

He bit into a biscuit and shook his head. "Nope, not

yet. But I slid pretty good last night on the way to Mr. Williams's property."

Sensing gossip—exactly what Dean intended—she leaned in and raised her eyebrows. "Old man Williams?"

"One and the same." He smiled—*Old man* Williams was only a few years older than Mrs. Booth.

"That old kook. Man's crazier than a ding bat. What was he calling about?"

"Thought he saw some trespassers on his land."

"Really?"

Dean nodded, sipped his coffee, and went in for the kill. "While I was out that way, I passed the old Novak Estate. I heard Earl's son had just gotten married and moved back."

She nodded enthusiastically. "Yep, true story. Clint moved back about six months ago. Came in here a few times with that new wife of his." She wrinkled her nose. "I never did like the kid too much. Spoiled brat, but you didn't hear that from me. Now, that new wife of his," she blew out a whistle. "Whoowie, is she a looker."

He did his best to remain aloof. "Really? Who is she?"

"Name's Heidi, sweet thing. Got kind of a hippie, earthy-type vibe from her, but whatever. She's a psychologist, specializing in criminals or something. Clint made a joke that she had to leave her clinic in West Virginia because one of her clients was totally obsessed with her or something."

Interesting.

She continued, "Eve says she's as sweet as honey, but quiet. Keeps to herself a lot."

"Eve?"

"Their live-in maid and personal chef. Young gal."

He raised his eyebrows. Heidi hadn't mentioned anyone else living at the house.

"Live-in?"

"Yeah, Eve, Jesse, Trevor. The Novak's have a full-time staff; you didn't know that?"

What the *fuck*? Why didn't Heidi tell him? He would have interviewed them immediately. For all he knew, they could have seen the son of a bitch that shot at Heidi, and him.

"No, I didn't. You're sure they live with her? The Novak's, I mean."

"I don't know if they all live there full-time, but Eve and Jesse do, for sure. They came in here just the other morning. They don't live *inside* the house with Heidi and Clint, they live about a quarter mile past it, out on the Novak's land. Three little stone cabins, built for the staff when the house was originally built in the 1920s."

Dean couldn't believe Heidi had left out that little, *huge*, piece of information.

"Must be nice to have staff."

Mrs. Booth rolled her eyes. "Can you imagine? Just wish that boy wasn't so spoiled. Never like to see that."

"I hear he's a dentist?"

The front door opened.

Mrs. Booth yelled across the diner. "Mornin' Sue, sit where you like, I'll get your coffee." She turned back to him. "Yep, just like Earl wanted."

"What do you mean?"

"Earl kept Clint and his sister, Julie, on a tight leash.

79

Like puppets, they were. Told them what to do, who to be. Used his money and influence to keep 'em in line." She shook her head. "And a belt. Although… Earl favored Clint over Julie, and everyone knew. Earl wanted only boys and was disappointed with a girl, or so the rumor was. Julie had it pretty bad. Anyway, after their mom died, those two were all they had. They're best friends."

"And where is she now, the sister?"

"Not sure, lives up north somewhere. She kinda disappeared after high school. Didn't really have any friends or anything, so nothing keepin' her here, I reckon. Clint's ten years older than she is, you know. I heard she and her husband are having financial difficulties, but who knows if that's true."

"Financial difficulties?"

"Yep, that's what I heard."

"Earl died of a heart attack, correct?"

"Yep, poor thing."

Dean sipped his coffee. "Where did the family get their money?"

"Earl's dad, their grandfather, was a wealthy banker with lots of family money, and Earl became a stockbroker. Was in New York a lot; hell, most of the time, I think. He hit it big during the internet boom. Or so I hear. He left everything to his kids… a lot to inherit."

"Equal amount to both?"

"*No*, I hear Clint got the lion's share of it."

"What about the wife? Do you know if they had a prenup or anything?"

Mrs. Booth raised her puffy eyebrows. "Ironclad prenup, and the rumor is that she waived her right to any of Clint's money."

Dean couldn't hide the shock on his face. He'd heard a lot of things in his life, but never a woman with a humble background, marrying a rich man and signing away all financial rights. It surprised him enough that he was at a loss for words. Of, course, he'd need to confirm the information.

The front door opened again, this time a duo of brave hunters coming in for a hot breakfast before an icy hunt.

"Well, dear, I've got to go make my rounds. Your breakfast will be out in just a minute."

"Thanks, Mrs. Booth."

She sent him a wink before walking away and Dean glanced out the window, in deep thought.

Lots of things bugged him about the conversation he'd just had with Mrs. Booth, but some more than others. One, why the hell hadn't Heidi mentioned her staff; two, who was this obsessed client of Heidi's back in West Virginia; and three, considering Heidi's prenup, exactly how much money does Clint's sister stand to inherit now that her dear brother is dead?

CHAPTER 9

DEAN STOPPED AT the base of the Novak's driveway, shoved the truck into park and got out.

Golden beams of morning light shot through the tall, ice-covered trees. A thick layer of ice coated the ground beneath his boots. The sleet had stopped, thank God, but according to Dan the weatherman, another round of ice and possibly a foot of snow was on its way. He'd be working overtime, no doubt about that.

Dean zipped up his jacket and looked around. The driveway was steep and narrow, with no view of the house from the base of it. Deep ditches ran along each side of the driveway, and just past that, dense woods. The only place to park a car would be the middle of the road, which he didn't think the shooter would risk.

A cold gust of wind swept up his back as he turned and walked to the other side of the dirt road. More of the same—ditches, woods. He surveyed the sides of the road, around the iron mailbox and the base of the driveway. No footprints, tracks, nothing.

Where the hell did the shooter come from?

He spent the next thirty minutes walking up and down the dirt road, looking for any signs of recent activity.

None.

He jumped in his truck and cranked up the heater. Dammit, it was cold.

The wheels spun out as he began to accelerate up the steep driveway. He reversed, shoved the truck into four-wheel drive and lightly pressed the accelerator.

As the old Chevy inched up the driveway, he took his time to look around. The grounds looked different in the morning light, less ominous. The farther up he drove, he noticed areas where the thick brush had been cleared out, leaving a manicured lawn dotted with dozens of trees. He leaned forward and peered through the windshield to where he assumed the shooter had set up shop. Lots of trees to hide behind, but still risky.

A sparkle caught his eye and he noticed a wind chime dangling from a tree. And, as he looked around, he saw at least six more. The large chimes looked as out of place as the suncatcher hanging in the kitchen. He smiled—must be more of Heidi's contribution to the estate.

Finally, he reached the top of the driveway and rolled to a stop behind Hayes's patrol car.

Hayes wasn't in it.

Dean rolled his eyes and got out.

The early light reflected off the ice that covered the stone mansion. The old house was actually sparkling.

Suddenly, he saw a flash of brown from the corner of his eye, followed by wild barking. Instinctively, he spun on his heel, his right hand sliding to the hilt of his gun. He locked eyes with the beast, ready to react to whatever wrath Gus was about to lay down on him.

As the coonhound drew closer, he slowed, and to Dean's shock, his tail began wagging. Dean raised his eyebrows, released his gun and waited to be approached.

The barking stopped as Gus sauntered up and casually began sniffing Dean's boots.

"We're progressing leaps and bounds, aren't we?" He bent over and ruffled the dog's ears.

As Gus spotted a bird and darted across the lawn, Dean walked up the porch, noting that the plastic that Hayes had stapled over the windows had held up through the night. He rang the doorbell.

A few seconds of silence passed so he rang again.

Nothing.

He frowned and glanced over his shoulder. Where the hell was everybody?

He rang again.

Fuck this.

He turned the knob. Unlocked.

The heavy door creaked open and as he stepped inside, he heard muffled voices across the house.

He glanced up the staircase as he walked past it, hoping to see Heidi walking down in another faded concert T-shirt and tight jeans.

No luck.

He glanced from room to room as he walked down the hall and finally into the kitchen, where Hayes was grinning from ear-to-ear, helping a busty blonde whip up a batch of pancakes.

Dean cocked an eyebrow, crossed his arms and leaned against the doorway.

"Good to know I'm not an intruder, Officer Hayes."

The spoon in Hayes's hand dropped to the floor, splattering mix all over the counters as he spun on his heel, his eyes the size of golf balls.

Dean had to keep from laughing as Hayes stuttered out an excuse.

"I, uh, was just helping, uh, Miss Eve here, sir." He cleared his throat, composing himself. "Sorry, sir, I just came in for a minute."

After giving Hayes a "gotcha" look, he looked at the woman in the apron, with her long blonde hair braided down her back and deep, tired circles under her blue eyes. Aside from the stress written all over her face, she was as cute as a button and, obviously, Hayes had taken notice.

"I'm Detective Dean Walker, BSPD." He met her across the room and they shook hands.

"So nice to meet you." She wiped her hands on her apron and exhaled. "I'm so glad you're here. I'm Eve, The Novak's maid and personal chef."

"Nice to meet you, Miss…"

"Schneider."

"Miss Schneider, do you live full-time with the Novak's?"

"Yes, in a cabin just down the hill."

Perfect—he mentally crossed off meeting the first staff member from his list. He looked past her at the mess on the kitchen counter. "When you have a spare second, I'd like to ask you a few questions."

"Of course. I'm just in the middle of getting breakfast going." She looked down, her eyes saddened. "Heidi doesn't have an appetite right now, but I'm hoping my pancakes will change her mind. And, um, Officer Hayes offered to help in exchange for a plate."

Dean glanced at Hayes who smirked and innocently shrugged.

"Would you like some? There's plenty. It would be my pleasure."

Although he'd just had breakfast, he knew that sitting casually around the table would be a perfect chance to get to know Miss Schneider better, and hopefully, gain some insight on the rest of the staff, and how the house operated. So he smiled and said, "No Southern man can resist a stack of homemade pancakes, Miss Schneider."

She clapped her hands together and smiled. "Great! Give me about twenty minutes."

Just then, behind him, he heard Heidi's voice. *"Alright then, see you soon."*

He turned, his heart skipping a beat when he saw her. She clicked off her cell phone, looked up and her eyes widened slightly as she saw him. Surprise? Relief? Something else?

"You made it." She smiled.

She wore a simple, white sweater over skinny jeans, with a small tear at the knee, tucked into furry winter boots. Her brown, curly hair was pulled back, with loose strands cascading around her face. She wore a necklace with small crystals around her neck. Her blue eyes looked tired and reflected a sleepless night.

He stepped out of her way. "Roads aren't too bad." He smiled. "Good morning."

She smiled bigger and something in her tired eyes sparkled. "It's good to see you, detective." She held his gaze for a moment, then her face darkened. "Do you have news?"

"Not yet..." He paused, suddenly noticing the red marks on the side of her face and neck. He stepped forward, closer. "What—

"Oh, just from the glass. It's nothing." She covered the marks with her hand and rubbed her neck, as if embarrassed by the battle wounds.

He felt a rush of anger pulse through his blood. She'd been hurt. The son of a bitch hurt her. He'd been wearing a coat and pants when the windows shattered, but she was only in a light robe. He should have been more thorough and checked her over. *Dammit.*

He felt the stare of Eve and Officer Hayes behind him.

Heidi cleared her throat, set her phone on the table and walked to the coffee maker. "Would you like some?"

"Please. Thank you."

As she poured two cups of coffee, she glanced over her shoulder at Eve. "Julie will be here soon."

Eve turned, surprised. "What? How did she get here so soon?"

"I guess she was already in town, well, the next town over, meeting with some artists for her shop up in Vermont. She wants to feature artists from her hometown, I guess."

"She didn't come by? Did you know she was in town? Didn't she call?"

Heidi quickly glanced at Dean, then back down at the coffee. "No, she didn't. I didn't know she was here."

"That's so odd. I wonder why she wouldn't stop by first. Did Clint see her? Before... you know."

Heidi walked over to Dean and handed him a *Princeton* cup filled with coffee. Hers was tie-dyed with a peace sign. "Cream or sugar?"

"Black."

She turned back to Eve. "I don't know."

Interesting. Meeting Clint's grieving sister was now pushed to the top of his list.

Eve stood still for a moment, obviously perplexed that Clint's sister had come to town without letting them know, then went back to making breakfast.

Heidi leaned against the counter.

Dean sipped his coffee, savoring the high-dollar flavor, and watched her for a moment. He remembered the morning after his father had been shot between the eyes. He was dazed, as if his brain couldn't possibly digest that he had just lost his father. He wouldn't speak, he wouldn't eat, he wouldn't drink. It wasn't until he saw his mother cry for the first time that he snapped out of it and realized that he wasn't the only one in pain. From that moment forward, helping his mother cope became his number one priority and his grief was replaced with an unrelenting rage that still gripped him to this day.

Suddenly, from the corner of his eye he saw movement outside the window—a figure emerging from the dark woods. Like lightning, he grabbed the Glock on his hip and in two swift steps, he jumped in front of Heidi; his body a shield.

Hayes spun on his heel, looked at Dean, then followed Dean's gaze out the window.

Eve leaned up from the oven and gasped at the gun in Dean's hand. "Oh, my God, what's going on?"

He felt the tug of Heidi's hand on his shirt and the warmth of her body as she stepped closely behind him, her fear palpable.

Hayes drew his gun and swiftly crossed the room to the patio door.

Eve glanced outside. "Guys, wait, that's just Jesse."

"Who's Jesse?" He heard Heidi exhale in relief behind him. He released the grip on his Glock and slid it back into the holster.

"He's our ranch hand. One of them, anyway. It's okay."

Still shielding Heidi, Dean relaxed his stance but his gaze stayed laser-focused on the young man walking across the patio.

Eve continued, "Haven't seen Trevor yet today."

Hayes stepped away from the door, but kept his eyes on Jesse as he walked back over to Eve.

The back door opened and the tall cowboy immediately took notice of the two officers standing in the kitchen. Wearing a beanie, thick overalls and a camo jacket, his brown eyes were as shaded as Heidi's and Eve's, and his face just as pale.

His gaze darted over to Eve and lingered on Hayes for a moment. Dean took notice. Then Jesse looked at Heidi, who had unwedged herself from behind Dean.

He walked over and hugged her. "How you doing?"

"Morning, Jesse, I'm doing okay, how are you?"

He didn't answer, and instead, turned to Dean and stretched out his hand. "Jesse Reid."

They shook hands. "Detective Dean Walker."

"Any news?"

"Not yet, but I'd like to speak with you this morning if you have time."

He spread his arms. "Now works just fine."

"Great."

"You two can go in the den if you'd like," Heidi said.

Jesse tore off his beanie revealing dark, shaggy hair that curled just behind his ears, and a tanned neck from too much time in the sun. He had a wide gait and a slight hunch in his back, which surprised Dean considering the kid looked to be in his mid-twenties. He led Dean into the den and motioned to a small seating area, next to a bay window.

Jesse sank into an oversized chair and Dean couldn't help but notice how comfortable he seemed, when most people instinctively tense up when speaking to law enforcement.

Dean sat across from him.

"Jesse Reid, you said?"

Jesse nodded, sat back and crossed his ankle over his knee.

"Don't recall the name. Are you from here?"

"Born down south, moved here when I was eight."

Dean didn't remember ever meeting Jesse, but the kid was at least a decade younger than him, so it wasn't surprising that they hadn't crossed paths.

"How long have you worked for the Novaks?"

He looked up, scratched his chin. "Going on three years. Earl hired me, and after he died, Clint kept me on."

"Do you live with them?"

"Yes, sir. Free rent in return for work."

"Were you here last night?"

Jesse's fists clenched. "Yeah." He blew out a breath. "I can't believe I didn't hear it—didn't wake up."

"Hear what?"

"The gunshots." He shook his head, uncrossed his leg and leaned forward. He was edgy now. Angry. "I just can't fucking believe this, detective. 'Scuse my language."

"A day doesn't go by without me hearing 'fuck', Jesse. Don't worry about it." He paused, allowing the silence to linger, knowing that Jesse would break first.

He did.

"I just don't know who would do this to Clint, and then shoot at Heidi? I mean, what the hell?"

"Lay out last night for me."

"I did my usual evening rounds, checking the horses, cows, fences, making sure the barn and sheds were locked up and then I went home, drank a beer, watched ESPN and fell asleep. I woke up this morning and about shit myself when I saw a patrol car out front."

"Were you alone?"

"When?"

"Last night?"

"Yeah, I guess I was."

"All night?"

He cleared his throat, uncomfortable now. "Yes."

"This morning?"

"Yes."

"Okay. When you were out checking things last night, did you see anyone on the land at all?"

"No, I don't recall."

"What about during the day?"

He thought for a moment. "No, just Eve." He glanced

toward the kitchen. "And Trevor and Heidi. We don't get much traffic out here; vehicle or foot."

"Hunters?"

"No, everyone around here knows this land belongs to the Novaks."

"Where had you been before you came in just a minute ago?"

His eyes narrowed, his cheeks flushed. "Walking the damn grounds looking for the son of a bitch."

Dammit. Now Jesse's tracks would be all over the damn place, potentially covering, or mixing with, the shooter's. This kid just made his job a hell of a lot harder.

"Find anything?"

"Not a damn thing."

"Were you and Clint close?"

Jesse inhaled, sat back. "Yeah, he'd kinda become like a brother to me over the last year. Kinda lonely out here alone all the time, ya know?"

"I bet. No girlfriend?"

Jesse rolled his eyes. "Girls are nothing but trouble."

Dean smiled—another one bites the dust. "Who else was here last night?"

"I'm not sure if anyone was in the house, but Eve was home," he glanced toward the kitchen, again, and this time began anxiously tapping his thumb on his knee. He turned back to Dean. "And I know Trevor was here earlier in the day."

There was definitely a story with him and Eve.

"How long have you known Eve?"

Something sparked in his eyes. "A few years."

"Y'all close?"

"I guess. Friends."

Dean dug deeper, looking for more of a reaction. "She single?"

Jesse's head snapped up. "Yeah, she is."

"Nice gal."

"Yep."

A moment ticked by.

"Trevor doesn't live here, is that correct?"

Jesse shook his head.

"Where does he live?"

"Apartments in town."

"Where is he now?"

Jesse shrugged.

That was alright he'd track Trevor down later today. He leaned forward. "Jesse, do you know who would want to kill Clint and Heidi?"

Jesse's eyes darkened. "I have no damn idea, but I intend to find out."

"How do you plan to do that?"

"Well... I'll look for him, I guess. The Novak's have been like a family to me, sir."

"I understand, but you leave finding whoever did this to me, do you understand?"

Jesse narrowed his eyes and as he started to open his mouth, Eve stepped into the room. "Breakfast is ready, boys."

The room sat silent for a second. Jesse shook his head, agitated, and stood. Dean pushed out of the chair, his six-foot four-inch body blocking Jesse's way. He reached into his pocket and gave him a card.

"You give me a call if you see or hear anything... or remember anything else."

Jesse nodded and sidestepped him.

"And Jesse?"

The ranch hand stopped, turned.

"Don't go all Rambo on me."

Jesse nodded and as he walked out of the room, Dean couldn't ignore the pit in his stomach.

CHAPTER 10

HEIDI'S HEART POUNDED softly in her chest as she leaned against the frosty windowsill, watching Dean's determined, focused gaze survey the icy wonderland outside.

Her body was flooded with emotions, still edgy from being shot at the evening before.

She took a deep breath. What would she tell her clients to do in times of total duress? To acknowledge the emotions; to accept the emotions and to address them. But that seemed impossible right now. Her head was spinning, anxiety coursed through her veins. If she stopped to allow herself to think—to think about her murdered husband, to wonder why someone would want her dead, and to begin to address all the things she needed to do to prepare for the funeral, she feared she'd break down.

And yet, of all the things she should be doing at that moment, there she was, staring out the window, watching the most beautiful man she'd ever seen in her life as he attempted to solve the biggest mystery of her life.

There was something about him that she couldn't quite

put her finger on. Beyond the hard exterior, there was an understanding behind his eyes, an understanding of her situation, and there was comfort in that. There was also a protectiveness that made her heart leap out of her chest. She'd seen it in his eyes after shielding her from the bullets, and she'd seen it twice already this morning when he'd noticed the cuts on her face, and perhaps most of all, when his massive body stepped in front of her, protecting her from the stranger he'd seen through the window. She'd felt so small and vulnerable hovering behind his strong body, and when she'd stepped closely to him, she'd grabbed the back of his shirt—a nonverbal begging for him to keep her safe. Safe from whatever harm was stalking her. As she stood safely behind him, she'd smelled him—that indescribable smell of man that made her want to melt. Melt into his muscular, protective arms.

She sipped her coffee. What the hell was she doing? Her husband's body wasn't even cold for Christ's sake! She was being absolutely ridiculous, and a cold-hearted bitch on top of it.

She stepped back from the window as guilt began to replace the lust brewing in her body. Shouldn't she be upstairs, balled into a corner, crying her eyes out? Shouldn't she be inconsolable, surrounded by tissues and wedding pictures? Shouldn't she be completely devastated, instead of lusting over someone she'd just met?

And then, a sick feeling knotted in her stomach. Had she ever even lusted over Clint? Hell, did she even really know her husband?

The doubts had started creeping up the moment they'd begun planning the wedding. Doubts about him, about marriage, about his lifestyle. But she'd gone with it, right down the aisle with two hundred people watching—only four of which belonged to her.

All four of which had expressed concern about her upcoming nuptials.

She was jerked from her thoughts by the sound of footsteps coming into the room.

"Mrs. Novak?"

She turned to see Trevor standing in the doorway. Concern shone from his eyes as he crossed the den.

"How are you doing?"

She turned from the window and blew out a breath. "Hey, Trevor. I'm doing okay. How are you?"

Pushing forty, Trevor was the first ranch hand Clint's father had hired, full-time, to help with the land. He was a shy, quiet workhorse with long, sandy blonde hair that he kept pulled back in a ponytail, crystal blue eyes and tanned skin that told a story of too many hours in the sun. He wasn't particularly large, but was thick as a bull. Muscles from fifteen hours of manual labor a day, she supposed.

He glanced out the window at Dean. "Have they found anything?"

She shook her head. "Not yet. The detective is searching outside. Oh, and I know that he wants to talk to you today."

"I assumed so." He shifted his weight. "If you need anything... anything at all, just let me know, okay?"

"Thank you."

"I'll be tending to the horses this morning, and will come in for a bit after that."

"Sounds good, Trevor."

As he walked out of the room, Heidi glanced back outside. She took a deep breath to ease her pulse and just as she started to turn from the window, Dean turned and looked directly at her. His eyes locked on hers, butterflies danced in her stomach, and she imagined him telling her that he would keep her safe.

* * *

Dean felt eyes on him, and he knew it was her.

His heart skipped a beat as he met her gaze through the frosty window.

Behind the exhaustion in her blue eyes, he saw something else. A twinkle of longing and desire; a need for something from him.

I'm right here; you're safe.

His stomach danced and he forced himself to look away.

What the hell was he doing? Her husband had been killed not twenty-four hours earlier and there he was, lusting after her, unable to ignore the electricity between them. Did she feel it, too? It felt like a magnet between them, an undeniable pull that was impossible for each of them not to feel. But what scared him the most was that it was more than just an attraction; it was something else. Deeper, much deeper.

Like a dagger through the heart.

He shook his head. Regardless of what was going on between them, she was in a vulnerable state and probably going through one of the hardest times of her life. It would be wrong of him to make any kind of advance, whatsoever.

He would not take advantage of her in a time of weakness, no matter what.

He needed to get a fucking grip, and control whatever emotions this woman was stirring up deep inside him.

He took a deep breath, the cold air burning his lungs. As he started to walk forward, he heard footsteps behind him.

"Detective."

He turned to see Heidi step onto the porch, zipping up a thick winter coat. She wore a beanie pulled over her curly brown hair and furry boots over her jeans. God, she was cute.

He fought it, but smiled. "What can I do for you ma'am?"

With a death grip on the iron railing, she carefully walked down the slick porch steps. "Found anything?"

He shook his head. "Was just about to head to the woods."

A cold gust of wind whipped through her long hair, sending her curls whipping around her face.

"What do you hope to find in the woods?"

"Tracks, trace evidence, bullet casings, you name it."

"Didn't you search last night?"

"Yes, but," he looked at her for a moment. "It's easy to miss things in the dark."

She glanced down at his hand. "What's that?"

"A metal detector."

She reached into her pocket and pulled out a pair of hot pink gloves. "I'd like to join you."

He raised his eyebrows. "It's twenty-six degrees out here."

She cocked her head, defiant. "You're out here, aren't you? And besides, a second pair of eyes can't hurt, right?"

Well, she had a point with that comment. He stared at her for a second and finally said, "Alright, but, my rules. You walk where I tell you, and don't walk where I tell you. And don't touch anything."

She raised her eyebrows, smirked, and with a slightly sarcastic tone said, "Yes, sir."

They started across the lawn, the ice crunching underneath their boots. The sunlight sparkled off the trees as they walked for a moment in silence.

"Thank you for having Hayes stay the night."

"Looks like he made himself right at home."

"I invited him inside early this morning. Don't beat him up over it."

Dean had already had a little chat with Hayes, reminding him to stay on the ball at all times. He liked Hayes but damn, the kid was like a puppy around attractive women.

She continued, "And, besides, it sure didn't look like Eve minded the help in the kitchen."

No, it looked like Eve was enjoying Hayes's company just as much as he was enjoying sneaking peeks under her low-cut T-shirt.

A few moments passed.

"I'd like to speak with Trevor today."

"He just got here. I told him you'd want to meet with him today. I told him everything."

"He's the only one who doesn't live on the property, correct?"

"Correct." She cleared her throat. "Well, sometimes he stays in the cabins, but he has an apartment in town."

She seemed embarrassed talking about her staff, which surprised him.

"How well do you know your staff?"

"First of all, I don't really refer to them as my staff." She wrinkled her nose. "It's so uncomfortable and impersonal... and so distant from the way I was raised." She took a deep breath. "Anyway, I know Eve the most, of course, being a woman. Earl hired her a few years ago. I have to admit, I was surprised at how young she is."

Dean glanced at her, reading between the lines. "Do you think she and Earl had something going on?"

She shrugged. "I'd hate to speculate."

Interesting.

"What about her and Jesse?"

Heidi shrugged. "He watches her a lot in my opinion, but I don't think the attraction is mutual."

He gazed into the woods, in deep thought. One thing was for sure—there was more to the Novak family, and the *staff*, than meets the eye. He had no doubt there were a lot of stones to uncover, but he had one thing nagging him that he needed to get to the bottom of, right now.

"Tell me about your clinic."

She smiled. "Smoky Quartz Center for Counseling. I was the go-to *head doctor*, as they called me, in my small town of Belle Ridge, and the surrounding towns, actually. It was great, just starting to really thrive."

"Smoky Quartz... because of the Smoky Mountains?"

"No, actually..." She slid him the side-eye and smirked. "Do you know anything about healing crystals, Dean?"

"Just the kind in the bags that I confiscate from drug dealers."

She rolled her eyes. "I'm not talking drugs, geez."

He grinned. "I know, but to answer your question, no, not really. Enlighten me... with your healing crystal talk."

"Alright, there are many stones and crystals that are said to have healing energies—

"Do you believe that?"

"Absolutely. Do you?"

He shrugged.

She continued, "Smoky quartz lays a protective shield against bad energy. It helps you let go and release things from the past, which cleans out your aura, and allows room for positive energy to enter the body and thrive. And that's probably the single most important thing for anyone who's seeking counseling for something." She glanced at him. "Let go of the past... let go of the pain and allow love and light in."

He immediately looked down, and thought of his father.

"Energy is all around us, you know. It's important to acknowledge that and be proactive about what you let into your body. I'm not stupid, Dean, I fully understand that holding a crystal in your hand will not solve your problems, but it gives my clients another way to look at the balance between positive and negative... in a tangible way. Which helps them wrap their heads around decluttering the negative things they hold onto, and allowing for happiness. Sometimes, people just need another way to look at things... and that opens up a whole new light. A healing light that they never even knew existed. A strength inside them, that they never knew existed."

"You miss it, your clinic." He said it as a statement, not a question.

"Yes, very much." She paused. "Since our plans changed and I moved here, I've played around with the idea of opening a clinic here."

"We could use a good head doctor here in Berry Springs."

"Every town could use a good head doctor."

"Do you specialize in one area, or is it all whack-jobs?"

She narrowed her eyes and grinned. "I'm glad to know how you feel about eight years of my education."

"Hey, I respect what you do and have seen it turn a lot of people's lives around. I just, personally, never really understood therapy, that's all." He paused. "Just handle your shit, ya know? Why do you need to sit on a couch and talk to a stranger about it?"

"Sometimes..." she looked up at him, "Other people can see deeper into you than you can see yourself. We're too close to see things, sometimes. It helps to have another set of eyes... kind of like what we're doing right now."

Touché.

He stepped off the lawn, where he had seen the tracks the night before, and into the woods, with her at his side. He stopped and glanced over his shoulder at the window that he and Heidi had been standing in front of when they had been targeted. Yep, if his instincts were correct—and he'd like to think that they were—this is the exact location where the shooter took aim.

Heidi continued, "And, to answer your question, yes, I specialized in young adults, delinquent juveniles, but had clients of all ages, all walks of life and all different kinds of problems."

He lightly grabbed her arm. "Don't walk here. Stay a few feet that way."

She nodded and stepped aside.

"Young adults? Half of all crimes are committed by teenagers and young adults in their twenties."

"Yes, I'm very aware of this."

"Must've had some interesting clients." He crouched down and slowly surveyed the ground, taking notice of a few freshly broken twigs.

Her voice lowered. "Just one."

He looked up at her, her sudden uncomfortableness was palpable.

"Tell me about him."

"Him, who?"

"The client." He looked back down at the ground, searching.

"Oh." She looked down for a moment. "He, um, Curtis Eagan, had a terrible childhood; abuse, the works. He was addicted to methamphetamines by age twelve—

"Oh, no, not smoky quartz."

She laughed. "Wow, a quick-witted, smartass detective. That's so cliché."

He grinned.

"Anyway, Curtis was in and out of juvie, and then jail. The judge ordered him to see me as part of his rehabilitation and sentencing, after he almost beat someone to death with a baseball bat." Her shoulders tensed. "It appeared that Curtis developed a crush on me, and it finally reached the point where I had to speak to the judge and they pulled him from my program."

Dean's instincts piqued. An obsessed, mentally deranged kid, kills husband of the doctor who he's in love with, then tries to kill the wife because she doesn't want him. Goosebumps prickled on his skin.

"What did he do? How did he show his feelings for you?"

"It started out with chocolates and flowers, sent to my office, but then he started sending letters—poems." She wrapped her arms around herself. "Creepy poems. And the last few times we spoke, I could just see... a look in his eyes. A look that made me want to jump out of the window."

Dean looked up, giving her his undivided attention now. His eyes narrowed. "Did you ever see him again? After the judge released him from your program?"

She shook her head. "No. No, never."

"Any contact, from him, at all?"

"No." She laughed softly. "I guess that was the only benefit of getting out of Belle Ridge. Anyway, I hope he finds his way, but my gut tells me that he's probably already locked up again."

He made a mental note to confirm Curtis Eagan's whereabouts for last night, immediately.

"Hey..." Her eyes locked on something on the ground and she bent over, peering closer. "Is that..."

He looked in the direction of her gaze. A gold beam of sunlight cut through the trees, twinkling off of something on the ground. Hope sparked as he pushed off the ground and carefully stepped over to the object.

He bent over and a rush of excitement shot through him.

Yes! A bullet casing.

"Good eye, doctor."

She smiled. "See? Two eyes are better than one."

"I'll agree once you find me the other four casings. There were five shots."

He pulled a tiny plastic bag from his pocket, plucked the brass from the ground and sealed it up.

"You're on."

A few minutes passed as they searched the surrounding area.

She was distracting him. Every few steps, he'd catch himself looking up at her, and he caught her doing the same. She was so beautiful in the early morning light. He wanted to take a picture of her. The way the light sparkled through her long curly hair that flowed past her hat. The way her skin looked like porcelain against the winter landscape, and her little pink nose, rosy from the cold. And the way she looked at him—the way she made him feel when she looked at him.

He shook the thoughts from his head and searched his brain for anything to get him back on the ball. "You mentioned something about Clint's sister coming in today?"

"Yes, she should be here anytime."

"Are you two close?"

She hesitated for a moment too long, and he knew he was about to uncover another Novak stone.

"Short answer—no, not really."

"Why?"

She walked a few steps before responding. "She and Clint were best friends. She's very possessive of him."

"She didn't like another woman stepping into his life?"

"I'd say that's an accurate statement."

"Was there a rift between you two?"

"No, no, not at all. She's always been cordial to me."

Cordial.

"And what about between her and Clint? Was she mad at him for marrying you?"

Heidi looked down. "I think so, yes."

Interesting.

"You said she was in town last night?"

"Right."

"But you didn't see her?"

"Right."

"Do you know where she was?"

She shot him a look. "Alright, I know where you're going with this and there's no way in hell she killed him, okay?"

He glanced over and raised his eyebrows. "I never said she did."

"That's where you're going with these questions, right?"

Just then, their attention was pulled to a red sports car speeding up the driveway.

"Speak of the devil."

CHAPTER 11

DEAN SLID THE plastic bag with the bullet casing in his pocket as the car skidded to a stop at the top of the driveway.

Heidi released an exhale, so faint that he might not have caught it if he hadn't been tuned into her reaction of seeing her beloved sister-in-law.

The door of the car swung open as Heidi made her way up the hill, with Dean on her heels.

Dean took a mental note of the make and model of the car as the five-foot-three, blonde-haired, blue-eyed disheveled woman in a designer coat scrambled out of the front seat. She spotted Heidi, and instead of running to her sister-in-law and embracing in a warm hug, Julie stood by the car, waiting for Heidi to come to her.

Dean noticed a change in Heidi's demeanor immediately—her whole body tensed.

Once they topped the hill and stepped onto the driveway, the two women still did not embrace. He was shocked by the coldness between them. Was this family? One had just lost her brother, and the other, her husband. Did that not warrant a sympathetic hug?

Heidi stepped up to Julie, her eyes somber but her body rigid.

"Hi Julie."

"Hey."

"I won't ask how you're doing."

"Thanks." Julie popped the trunk and walked around the car.

Just then, Gus barreled down the driveway, barking wildly at the newcomer. Julie's back straightened like a rod as the dog drew closer.

Having been on the receiving end of Gus's welcome multiple times in the last twenty-four hours, Dean grinned as Heidi attempted to grab the ball of fur barreling down the driveway.

Gus bolted past her and skidded to Julie's feet, barking like a maniac, and as the dog crouched to leap, Julie threw her hands up—her designer purse flying out of her hand—and squealed.

Dean had to bite his lip to keep from laughing.

"No Gus, *no*." Heidi grabbed Gus's collar, pulled him back, and Dean swore he saw a small smirk cross her lips.

"It's okay, buddy, it's just Julie."

"*Dammit*, that damn *dog*, Heidi." Julie picked up her alligator-skin purse and brushed it off. "That *damn, damn, damn,* dog.

"Sorry. He's a little shaken up with all the activity."

"Well, so the fuck am I." She blew out a breath. "Damn dog. Damn dogs in general. Don't know why any-one would want an animal around that just sheds hair all over the damned place all day." Now more disheveled than ever, she leaned into the trunk.

Apparently, Dean was invisible to the woman.

He stood back, watching the icy interaction and raised his eyebrows as Julie handed Heidi a piece of her luggage. Heidi's cheeks flushed as she slid him a glance to see if he'd noticed her sister-in-law's insulting gesture. Yeah, he'd definitely noticed. So as any gentlemen would do, he walked over, tugged the luggage from Heidi's hand and stepped next to Julie.

"Can I help with that?"

Julie turned and stared at him for a moment.

"Who're you?"

"Detective Dean Walker, BSPD."

Her eyes rounded. "Oh. Sorry." She squinted, cocked her head. "Wait a second, *Dean Walker?*"

"Yes, ma'am."

"Holy shit, you were just a few years older than Clint in school, weren't you? Well, maybe more than a few."

He nodded.

"And you're, what, close to ten years older than me, right?"

"Close to that."

"Sorry, I didn't see you, and I didn't realize you were a detective now. Sorry."

"Nothing to be sorry about. Here, how about I take that from you?"

"Thanks." Julie proceeded to pull two more bags from the trunk. It never ceased to amaze him how much a woman could pack for a single trip. Especially this woman.

If he had to guess, he'd bet his life that one of the bags was filled with shoes—only shoes.

Julie put her hands on her hips and looked up at him as he struggled with the bags.

"Where are we with the investigation, Detective Walker? Have you found who murdered my brother?"

Dean straightened, his body towering over hers. He didn't like this woman, not one bit.

"We're working on it; we've put all resources into finding out who did this." And with a hint of sarcasm, he asked, "Where would you like your luggage, ma'am?" He caught Heidi grin for a split second before her face hardened again.

Julie narrowed her eyes. Apparently, she didn't care too much for him, either.

In an attempt to dissolve the mounting tension, Heidi took one of the bags from Dean's hands and turned to her sister-in-law. "Your room's ready, and Eve got you your favorite wine."

"I could use a glass right now." She turned and walked into the house—with only her purse on her arm. Dean noticed that she pushed through the front door and hung up her coat and purse, as if the house still belonged to her.

"Just set the bags right there, thanks."

The trio stood awkwardly in the hall for a moment, and finally, Dean broke the ice.

"Julie, I'd like to talk to you for a few minutes, if you don't mind."

Julie took a deep breath. "Would you mind if I got settled first? I'm sorry... I'm so shaken up. I just need a minute."

He nodded. "Understandable. I'll give you some time, then." He handed her his card. "But please feel free to call me anytime if you think of anything, or if you're ready to talk before I see you again."

She took the card, slid it into her pocket. "Thanks."

He glanced at Heidi, and caught her staring at him. She quickly looked down and shifted her weight.

"I'll give you ladies some privacy. Heidi, please call me if you need to. I'll see you soon."

She smiled. "Thank you."

He smiled, took another glance at Julie who was fumbling with her designer gloves, then pushed out of the front door.

* * *

"Cross here."

Dean gripped the steering wheel as his truck slid around a tight turn. The sunny morning had turned into a dark, dreary afternoon with thick clouds hanging low in the sky, threatening more sleet.

"Wesley, hey, it's Dean."

"Hey man, what's up?"

"Just pulling dumbasses from ditches."

"It's slick as shit outside, I bet y'all are busy as hell."

Busy as hell didn't even cover it. Dean would have been busy in this weather without dealing with a homicide—*correction*—a homicide *and* attempted murder. He'd left the Novak Estate for the police station over two hours ago—a drive that should have taken him thirty minutes, had taken him four times that. It was already close to lunchtime and his stomach growled relentlessly, reminding him every few minutes.

"Just wish people would stay off the damn roads."

Wesley chuckled. "Tell Davis to close down the liquor store then."

A former Marine, Wesley Cross owned and operated a small arms dealership where he had just begun manufacturing his own firearms—Cross Combat. The business started out as a hobby but had grown quickly over the last few years. Wesley and Dean had been friends since grade school, and although Wesley was a bit too cocky in Dean's opinion, the man could back it up, which Dean appreciated. Wesley was a muscular tank of a man, with short brown hair, blue eyes and a sharp jaw that made him look like he'd just stepped out of the latest superhero movie. And the women of Berry Springs definitely took notice. Something about Wesley made women crazy. Dean had recently arrested one of Wesley's ex-girlfriends for breaking and entering into his shop, trying to track him down after he'd quit returning her calls.

Looks aside, Wesley was also the town's ballistics expert which was exactly why Dean was calling him today.

"I've got a casing I need you to look at."

"This wouldn't be the one pulled from Clint Novak's brain, would it?"

"And where exactly did you hear that?" Damn department leaks, and damn the gossip.

"I will not reveal my sources."

"Ellen in dispatch."

"Yep."

"*Dammit.* Someone's got to sew that girl's lips shut."

"Just wait until after my date with her, will you?"

"You're joking."

"Hey, someone got shot between the eyes in our town. I needed to know who it was, and more importantly if one of my guns was found at the scene."

"No guns. But to answer your earlier question, this particular casing isn't the one from his head. You'll get that one after the autopsy."

"You found another one at the scene?"

"At a related scene."

"What the fuck? He shot someone else, somewhere else?"

"Attempted, and failed." He braked as he saw a trail of taillights ahead. "Dammit, got another accident on the mountain. I'll drop the slug off today. Need to know the type of gun it came from."

"You got it, man. Hey, keep me up to date, will ya?"

"Will do."

Click.

Dean flicked on his lights rolled to a stop behind a beat-up Chevy, which was the fourth vehicle in a line of cars halted on a narrow two-lane road that snaked through the mountains.

He grabbed his hat from the passenger seat, pulled on his gloves and stepped out of the car. The dense clouds above made the thirty-degree temperature seem colder than it actually was.

Black puffs of exhaust rolled from the tail pipes as he passed the cars, one by one.

He reached for his radio.

"Dispatch, I need someone sent to my location to direct traffic."

"10-4 Officer Walker."

"And Sandy? Tell Ellen to keep her mouth shut."

A crackled laugh. "I do every damn day, Dean."

Dean walked up to the rusted blue Honda that was sticking halfway out of the ditch. The window was fogged up as he tapped on it.

From inside, a hand wildly wiped the condensation and a small face framed by long blonde hair and wide, panicked eyes peered out.

Dean cocked an eyebrow as she rolled down the window.

"Oh, *Detective Walker*, I'm *sooooo* glad to see you."

"Eve, looks like you've got yourself in quite a pickle." He smiled, to ease her.

She nodded feverishly and tears began to fill her eyes. "I just... I needed to run to the grocery store, and thought I could make it. But... I ran off the road. Obviously."

"Obviously."

She looked in the rearview mirror. "They've been honking like crazy, I didn't know what to do."

Like a hawk, Dean spotted the barrel of a revolver sticking out from under her purse on the passenger seat.

He tensed. "Eve, is that gun you have on your passenger seat loaded?"

Her eyes bugged, her mouth dropped. For a moment, she said nothing, and then finally, "Um, yes, sir. It belongs to the Novak's. Um, Earl gave it to me last year."

Why the hell would Earl give his maid a gun?

Nervous as a puppy, she rambled on. "You know,

they have a big collection, and well, one day he taught me to shoot. And he gave it to me. I carry it in my purse sometimes."

"And why is it out of your purse and on the seat?"

She bit her lip. "All the honking, and I'm all alone, I just took it out. I've been scared."

"Is it loaded?"

"Yes, sir."

"Okay." He reached into the car, opened his palm. "How about if you give it to me for a second."

She nodded and her hand shook as she handed him the gun. Careful so that the cars behind them couldn't see, he quickly unloaded the gun and handed it back to her.

"Leave it unloaded for now, alright?"

She nodded.

"You'll need to get your license if you want to carry it, you understand?"

"Yes, sir."

Just then, behind him, he heard, "Detective Walker."

Dean turned to see Hayes walking briskly down the road.

"What the hell are you doing here? You're supposed to be home, getting some sleep."

Hayes's face flushed and Dean wasn't sure if it was from the weather or something else.

"Eve called me."

"*Eve* called you?"

"Yeah."

"For what exactly?"

"To come get her."

"She called you personally, or called the station and the call was forwarded to you?"

Hayes looked down and cleared his throat. "Personally. Sir."

Dean glanced over his shoulder. Shrinking in her seat, Eve watched them from the corner of her eye.

He looked back at Hayes and narrowed his eyes. "How does she have your personal cell phone number, Hayes?"

Pause. "I gave it to her."

"While you were peeking down her shirt and whipping up a stack of flapjacks in the Novak's kitchen?"

"Yes, sir."

Dean crossed his arms over his chest, taking a moment to contemplate how he should handle the situation. He had no doubt Eve was a wealth of information regarding Earl, Clint, Heidi and the staff, and that information could be very useful... no matter how it was obtained. Or to whom it was provided to.

He cocked his head and looked at the line of angry drivers. "Well, knight in shining armor, looks like you've got a fun few hours on your hands."

Hayes glanced back at the cars and his shoulders dropped, suddenly realizing that this wasn't going to be as easy as swooping in and saving the damsel in distress.

Dean grinned and slapped him on the back. "Have fun, son." As he turned to walk away he said, "And Hayes, get me that revolver."

* * *

"*Son of a bitch*, it's colder than a penguin's pecker out there."

Dean glanced up from his desk as Jameson stepped into his office and ripped off his thick winter gloves with his mouth. Between his teeth, he said, "I've pulled five people out of ditches already today."

Dean blinked the blurriness from his eyes and glanced at the clock. It was already three-thirty in the afternoon. After leaving Hayes to deal with the mess on the mountain, he'd stopped twice to check on abandoned cars on the side of the road, grabbed a bite to eat, then headed into the station where he'd been returning calls, taking calls, filling out reports and spending every spare second on the Novak murder.

It had already been a hell of a day.

"Dan the weather guy says there's more weather coming."

Dean leaned back, stretched his neck from side to side. "I saw that."

Jameson sank into the chair across from his desk. "So get me up to speed."

"Found a slug."

Jameson raised his eyebrows. "No shit?"

"No shit. Where the shooter staked us out."

"Just one?"

"Just one. Five shots. He must've cleaned up after himself, but missed one when I came after him."

"Where is it?"

"Dropped it off with Cross."

Jameson nodded. Although Cross was technically off the books, everyone in town knew that he was the best ballistics expert around. When BSPD needed ballistics evidence looked at immediately, they went right to him. It was a poorly kept secret that everyone knew, yet everyone understood—small town departments, with a major lack of resources, did what they had to do to get things done, and BSPD was no different. But because Wesley wasn't "official," his findings wouldn't hold up in court, so the evidence was always sent down to the State Crime Lab afterward for additional analysis, which took weeks.

"So who'd you chat with today?"

Dean inhaled and mindlessly picked up his pen. "The Novak's have a full-time staff of three—two ranch hands and a personal chef, who doubles as a maid. I met with all three today. Eve, the chef, possibly had an affair with Earl before he died. She also carries a revolver in her purse."

"Sounds like my kind of gal."

"No, she has a job." He grinned then continued, "Jesse's a young kid, mid-twenties, and isn't taking the news very well. Seems he and Clint were pretty close. He was on the land during the shooting, but claims he didn't hear a thing. And Trevor, I met him on my way out. A real Southern cowboy, early forties. He's been with the Novak's the longest, but unfortunately, he didn't have much to say—at all. Quiet type. Says he wasn't there last night. I'm pulling security camera footage from his apartment building to confirm that."

"Sounds like a motley crew. What's your initial read?"

He squinted and shook his head. "There's a hell of a lot more to the Novak Estate than meets the eye, no doubt about it." He began tapping the pen on his desk. "Eve and Jesse live in cabins about a half-mile from the house and Trevor stays occasionally, apparently. There's three small stone cabins, lined in a row, backed up to the woods."

"Sounds quaint."

"Yeah, a little too quaint. Looks like elves and fairies should be dancing around. Eve and Jesse get free rent in exchange for work."

"Not bad. Does the main house have cameras?"

Dean rolled his eyes. "No. Earl's security was his gun arsenal."

"Sounds like a typical Berry Springs guy."

Dean let out a *humph* and then said, "Then I met the sister."

"Clint's sister?"

He nodded. "A sister who doesn't care much for Mrs. Novak, and is the sole heir to the Novak fortune now that Clint's dead." Dean pulled up a picture of Julie and flipped his computer monitor screen around.

Jameson cocked an eyebrow. "Not bad."

Nothing compared to Heidi.

"She's from here, right?"

"Yep, born and raised."

"You know her?"

"No, she's quite a bit younger than I am."

"Where does she live now?"

"Vermont. She stands to inherit Clint's fortune of nine-and-a-half million dollars."

Jameson blew out a whistle. "Nice chunk of change. But doesn't she have her own money? Didn't she get an inheritance when their dad passed?"

"She didn't inherit nearly as much as Clint. Earl's will was lopsided, significantly so. I've gotten wind that Earl favored his son over his daughter—quite the family rift. She got houses, cars, etcetera, and Clint got some mate-

rial things but mainly the stock options which had quadru-
pled since the will was written decades ago. He got all the
money. And get this; according to my research, the sister
and her husband had just filed bankruptcy."

"No shit?"

"No shit."

"Okay, there's motive there, but why kill Heidi too?
Unless..." Jameson leaned forward, resting his elbows
on his knees. "With the wife dead, the sister wouldn't
have to worry about her getting any of Clint's money."

Dean shook his head. "Nope, Heidi doesn't get a penny.
She signed an ironclad prenup, voluntarily. So I hear."

"You're shitting me."

"Nope."

"So if the wife wasn't going to get any of the money
anyway, why go after her?"

"Not sure on that one yet. Jealousy maybe."

Jameson shook his head. "Wow. So the sister, who's
in a financial pickle, and probably has been jealous of her
father's love for her brother her whole life, stands to inherit
millions now that her dear brother is dead."

"Yep. And—for the cherry on top—she just happened
to fly into town a few days ago, so she was here last night."

"No way. Shit man, bring her in for questioning."

"No, not yet. I need to check some things first."

"What if she skips town?"

"I've got her flagged at the airport."

"How the hell did you do that so quick?"

"An old friend."

Jameson cocked an eyebrow and grinned. "You mean
Wendy? Wendy the flight attendant?"

"One and the same."

Jameson gazed longingly up at the ceiling. "Man, was she hot. That was how long ago? What ever happened to her?"

"Distance. Anyway, I'll know the minute she checks in to leave anywhere."

"What about driving?"

"She's got a rental car from the airport, which I have all the information on. If she skips town, I'll find her. Anyway, I met her briefly. And I mean *briefly*. I was there when she arrived at the Novaks. She was a nutcase, like a wound-up Chihuahua. I was able to ask her a few casual questions but she told me she needed to rest, get a grip... it was obvious that she had no interest in talking whatsoever to a detective. And, side note, she was cold as ice to Heidi."

"You think she's jealous of her? Did she come off as the jealous type?"

"You could say that. Seems high-maintenance as shit." He paused. "You know those girls with real high-pitched voices that talk really fast and smell like a candy store?"

Jameson smiled. "Mmm-hmm."

"She's kind of like that. One of those."

"Is Heidi like that?"

"Oh, hell no, they're total opposites." He laughed. "Comically so."

"Where's the sister's husband?"

"Home, in Vermont."

"You verify that?"

"I'm working on it."

"Hey boys, cold as fuck, ain't it?" Jonas sauntered into Dean's office, sipping his lukewarm coffee.

A few years past thirty, Jonas's official title at the department was evidence tech, but his unofficial titles included information specialist and computer forensic analyst. He was as smart as a whip, especially with computers, and Dean often wondered why he didn't find a job that paid more than peanuts. Jonas was indispensable to the department; he knew it, and everyone else knew it, and because of that, McCord gave him the most leeway when it came to the rules. Jonas came and went as he pleased, but was always working. Whether it was in his tiny cubicle, or with an ice-cold beer on his sofa, the guy was always plugged in.

Jameson glanced over his shoulder. "Mornin'."

Dean nodded in salutation. "We were just talking about Julie Davis. Sit down."

"My timing is impeccable then." Jonas sat next to Jameson. "Looks like our little Barbie doll just opened an offshore account."

"You're fucking kidding."

"Nope."

"Where?"

"Switzerland."

Jameson rolled his eyes. "Such a cliché."

"I know."

Dean leaned forward. "Did she transfer anything into it?"

"Nope."

"Maybe just getting ready to receive ol' Clint's money."

"Maybe... how much did you say she and her husband have in assets? Currently."

"Aside from his income, seven hundred and thirty-two dollars in savings. And her art shop is a money pit."

Dean scribbled the number on his notepad. "Does she have any large withdrawals, recently?"

"Nope… nothing to make me think she hired someone to kill her brother. If that's what you're insinuating."

"Yes, that was what I was insinuating. Did you pull the husband's security footage?"

"Yep, I checked the security cameras at his office, and hacked into their home security—he's clean. He went straight to work, and then home last night. Was there all night."

Dean paused. "Okay, and you sent off the truck tracks from the cliff, and the soil sample from the Novak's porch?"

"Yep, this morning. Should hear something in the next day or two."

"Stay on it."

"Yes, sir."

Jameson's cell phone rang and he stood. "Well, boys, looks like we've got our prime suspect. I gotta take this." He answered his phone as he walked out of the office.

"Nice work, Jonas."

"Thanks, and I never told you, congratulations on becoming detective."

"Thanks, but it's not official yet—I think it's pass or fail on this case."

"I got faith in you, man."

Dean grinned. "That should do it then."

Jonas laughed.

"I need you to do something else for me."

"You got it."

"I need you to look into a Curtis Eagan for me."

"Who's Curtis Eagan?"

"A former client of Heidi's."

"From her psychology clinic in Belle Ridge?"

"Yep, Smoky Quartz Counseling—

"What the hell is smoky quartz?"

"I don't know, something about good and bad energy... or a shield... with soap... to clean out the body... I don't know. Anyway, this kid developed a little crush on her, and has a rap sheet. I want you to look into him, and also try to verify his whereabouts last night."

Jonas glanced at his nails. "And I thought you were going to give me a challenge."

"The day is young."

"In that case, I better get going."

CHAPTER 12

AYES GLANCED OVER at Eve as they bounced down the bumpy dirt road. She looked so little in the passenger seat of his patrol car... and embarrassed. She was all bundled up in an oversized winter coat that hung down to her knees, earmuffs and gloves. Dammit, she was the cutest thing he'd ever seen.

Beads of sweat began to form under his uniform. He reached forward and turned down the heat.

"You warm enough?"

She nodded. "I think I've finally thawed out."

It had taken two hours to pull her car from the ditch and clear traffic. He was tired, hungry and behind on work, but as he looked at her now, it was definitely worth it.

She looked at him, smiled, her blue eyes twinkling. "Thank you for taking me home."

"Not a problem. Just... stay off the road for a while, alright?"

She giggled, her cheeks flushed. "Oh, I won't be driving again for a while."

"Good."

"It's just past this corner up here, on the right. You'll see the dirt road."

Off in the distance, nestled along the winter landscape, were the Novak's three stone cabins.

"Mine is the far one, on the right. They're cute, aren't they?"

"They look like something you'd see on *Lord of the Rings*."

"I love it, and it's rent-free. Can't beat that."

"Nope, sure can't."

He rolled to a stop in front of the only cabin with outside decorations—painted pots with shrubs, candles, decorative frog rocks and a rocking chair next to a wicker table.

He shoved the car into park and looked over at her.

She began fidgeting with her keys.

His experience with women was limited, but one thing he knew was that a girl fidgeting with her keys before saying goodbye was always a good thing.

"Um, would you like to come in?"

Bingo. He glanced at the clock, pretending like he was contemplating—can't seem too eager now—and then nodded. The truth was, he'd miss a flight to Hawaii to go inside with this girl.

"Sure, maybe for a second." *Or, all night.*

She smiled and pushed out of the passenger door. "Great."

The winter wind whipped around him as he met her at the front of the car. She stepped ahead of him, onto the porch and slid her key into the lock.

He looked around. "So Trevor and Jesse stay at these cabins?"

She opened the door. "Yes, Jesse's is the one on the end and Trevor's is the middle. Trevor doesn't stay all the time, though."

He followed her into the cabin, which was small as hell but as thoughtfully decorated as the outside. He could see the entire place from the front door. The cabin was one large room with a tiny kitchen, a sitting area with couch and TV, a queen size bed flanked by dressers and, in the back corner, was what he assumed to be a bathroom and closet. The centerpiece of the cabin, though, was the beautiful stone fireplace in front of the bed.

Overall, it was quaint and cozy. And cute. Just like Eve.

She hung her purse on the coat rack and walked over to the fireplace. As she kneeled down and grabbed a piece of wood, he stepped over and took the wood from her hands. "I'll get it."

She smiled, their faces inches apart. "Thank you."

He locked eyes with her and for the first time, he noticed the cluster of freckles that dotted her cheekbones. As if she could be any cuter.

"Would you like something to drink?"

As she stood, he shoved the wood in the fireplace. "Sure."

"Coke, water, milk or tea. I'd offer you a beer but I'm assuming it's a bit too early for that."

It's never too early for beer, but he knew that Detective Walker would argue that, so he settled for a glass of tea instead. He began strategically stacking the wood in the fireplace when he noticed something in the ashes. He glanced over his shoulder, before leaning closer.

Burned pictures. Freshly burned from what he could

tell. He took another look over his shoulder, then leaned in, grabbed them, and stuffed them in his pocket.

The fire began crackling by the time she brought him his drink.

"Wow, thanks. I make a fire every single night and can never get it started that quickly."

"No problem." He sipped his tea, the sugar tickling his taste buds—nothing like a glass of sweet Southern tea, even in the dead of winter.

"So... do you—

His phone rang. *Dammit.*

He pulled it from his pocket, walked across the cabin for some privacy, and when he realized that there was none, he turned his back.

"Hayes here... where... how many cars... shit... okay, I'll be there soon."

He clicked off the phone and crossed the room—in three steps no less. "Duty calls."

"Damn weather."

He smiled. "Yes, damn weather, and damn women drivers thinking that they can drive in it."

She laughed and punched him in the arm. "Hey!"

"Just joking."

"You'd better be." She set her drink down. "I'll walk you out."

In a grand total of two steps, they were at the front door. She put her hand on the doorknob, turned to him, and paused.

Nerves tickled his stomach as he looked at her, the glow from the fire dancing in her blue eyes. She stared at him for a moment, and then smiled the sweetest smile. "Thanks again for everything."

She reached up on her tiptoes and kissed him on the cheek.

His eyes widened in surprise and then, as any warm-blooded male would do, he leaned down and kissed her right on the lips. A long, passionate kiss.

His pants began to tighten as he pulled away, his head spinning.

"Uh..." he struggled to find his words. "Uh, thanks for the drink."

She grinned and opened the door. "Anytime."

As he walked outside he glanced over his shoulder and said, "Stay off the roads, Miss Eve."

"Don't worry, I will."

He heard the door close behind him and as he walked to the car, he reached under his jacket and patted the revolver he'd swiped from her purse.

* * *

Dean smiled as he opened the front door. The smell of fresh lasagna—his favorite—and the soft fragrance of his mother's perfume scented his childhood home.

"My baby!" Wearing an apron that said *Mr. Goodlookin' is Cookin'*—an apron that once belonged to his father—his mother walked down the hall with arms wide-open for a hug.

At age seventy-one, Nancy was a five-foot-two ball of energy. She was as healthy as a horse and walked three miles a day, every day. Dean got his drive and restlessness from her, and his perseverance, looks and height from his dad.

"Hey, Mama." He smiled, hugged her and kissed her cheek. "Smells good."

"Your favorite. You hungry?"

He shook out of his jacket. "I could eat a hole in this house."

She frowned. "You've been busy, haven't you? Too busy." She grabbed his arm and led him into the kitchen.

"Not just me—the whole department's been busy but that's to be expected with slick roads and steep mountains... and idiots."

"More weather coming, you know. Supposed to be more ice, then a foot or more of snow."

He groaned. "Yeah, I've heard." He'd be even busier with another round of weather.

She grabbed an ice-cold beer from the fridge, popped the top and handed it to him. "And, on top of all that, you're working a homicide, Mr. Detective." She winked.

He took a deep sip, welcoming the cool, refreshing sizzle that slid down his throat. "Yeah, and this one isn't cut and dry."

A line of concern drew between her eyebrows as she began chopping tomatoes for the salad. She took a deep breath. "I heard he was shot between the eyes."

Dean's heart sank. It was the seven-year anniversary of his dad's death. Every year on this day, he and his mother had a big dinner and shared each other's company, to help ease the gloom of the day. And today, of all days, his mother had heard that Clint Novak had been shot between the eyes, just like her husband.

Dean set down his beer and walked over to his mother. "Do you need some help, Mama?"

She looked up at him. "Was he shot between the eyes?"

Dean nodded, grabbed a head of lettuce and began washing it in the sink.

She blew out a breath and shook her head. In a soft, sad voice she said, "Who would do something like that?"

Dean clenched his jaw. Nothing pissed him off more than seeing his mother upset, and it lit an even bigger fire under his ass to find whoever the hell did this.

"Well, Mama," he attempted to make his voice sound upbeat, "it's my job to worry about that kind of stuff so you don't have to."

"I worry about anything you worry about."

He grabbed her hand, turned her to him. "Not today, okay? You've made a nice dinner, I've got an ice-cold beer sitting on the table and you've got... where's your wine?" He looked around until he spied a glass at the end of the counter. "There it is. You've got a glass of wine. Let's be happy tonight and honor Dad the way he would want us to."

She smiled and stepped into his arms. "I love you so much, son. I don't know what I'd do without you."

"That makes two of us."

After another squeeze, she let go and waved him away. "Alright, you go sit at the table, take a load off. Dinner is almost ready."

He walked over to the table and sat down. "Bobby make it out today?"

"Of course. Everyone's good; the cows, the horses and chickens. He put the horses in the barn for the night—you know it's supposed to get down in the single digits tonight?"

"I heard. Won't do much for the ice that's still on the roads either."

He thought of Heidi and the front windows that were

loosely covered in plastic. He needed to make sure she got new windows put in STAT. Not only to block out the cold, but to block out someone who might want inside. He shifted in his seat. Just the thought of Heidi made him anxious and ancy.

The oven timer dinged and, with a smile on her face, his mother set a beautiful, bubbling lasagna on the table followed by a fresh salad and homemade garlic bread.

"Looks good Mama, thanks."

"Eat up. You look tired and worn down."

He smiled and loaded up his fork. "Yes, ma'am."

Thirty minutes and two slices of fresh apple pie later, Dean gulped the rest of his beer and pushed away from the table.

As he grabbed his plate, his mother stood. "Don't you dare. I'll clean up." She walked over to the liquor cabinet and pulled down a bottle of Irish whiskey—his father's favorite. "Go see Dad, like you always do."

He smiled and took the liquor from her. "I'm gonna take Dusty. I'll check on the other horses while I'm in the barn."

"Sounds good, sweetheart, take your time."

Dean nodded and after pulling on his coat, he walked outside.

Night had fallen and so had the temperatures. He stepped off the porch and glanced up at the sky. A thousand stars twinkled brightly around a full moon. It was a cloudless, clear night. His boots crunched on the ice that insisted on clinging to the ground as he walked around the house, the silver glow of the moon lighting his way. He glanced around. Ahead of him were acres and acres of fields, dotted with cattle. To his left and right, dense woods that looked like one big black mass in the night.

He knew every inch of this land by heart. This was his land. His land to watch over and protect.

Since joining the police department six years ago, he'd had less time to help out at the ranch, which is why Nancy had hired Bobby—a sixty-five-year-old cowboy and a long-time family friend. If Dean couldn't work the land every day, Bobby was the next best person. Dean also liked the idea of a man being around the house. Not that his mother couldn't take care of herself, but it just made him feel better that she wasn't alone, every day.

A cold gust of wind swept across his face as he cut through the field. A coyote howled in the distance. He glanced over his shoulder. Behind him, the house was lit and he could see his mother's silhouette in the kitchen. Washing dishes, probably. He turned, unlocked the padlock to the barn and pushed open the door.

The horses whinnied as he walked in.

"Hey, boys, gals."

Dean's mother had twelve horses. Among them were four quarter horses and two thoroughbreds that she bred, which brought in a nice chunk of change. But his favorite, was his horse, a brown mustang that he named Dusty.

"Hey, buddy."

Dusty nuzzled against his shoulder.

"Wanna go for a walk?"

Dean pulled Dusty from the pen, saddled him up and jumped on.

"Alright, buddy, let's go." He guided the horse out of the barn and into the dark night. He inhaled the cool win- ter air as Dusty leisurely stepped into the field.

He loved riding horses—something about it made him feel free; free of worry, free of stress. He closed his eyes for a moment and listened to sounds of the woods around him—the wind whispering through the tall pine trees, the sound of Dusty's hooves crunching on the icy grass beneath him and the night calls of the thousand different critters that call the Ozark Mountains home. The faint smell of a fire burning somewhere in the distance tickled his nose.

Despite the picturesque surroundings, he looked into the woods and tensed. Usually, being alone on his land cleared his head and gave him a calmness that only the outdoors could provide. But not tonight. Tonight, the woods seemed ominous in the dark night, with long shad- ows stretching across the field like fingers reaching for him.

Like someone watching him from the darkness, wait- ing to grab hold.

He thought of his mother, and the look in her eyes when she asked about Clint Novak. Although it wasn't said, there was no doubt that she had been thinking the same thing he had been since he looked down at Clint's body. Could it be the same person? The same person who killed his father six, now seven, years ago?

The thought seemed inconceivable. What was the connection between his father and Clint, and why wait seven years?

It wasn't just the location of the bullet hole; it was just something in his gut that made him on edge about it. A sixth sense. And obviously, something in his mother's gut felt the same way, too.

He pulled Dusty to a stop where just seven years ago—to the day—he and his father were burning brush, right before his father was shot and killed.

He sat still for a moment. His eyes scanned the tree line in the distance—as he had done a million times—trying to put a face to the murderer who killed his father. Was it someone who knew him? Or was it just pesky trespassers who got a little too trigger happy?

He took a deep breath and slid off the horse.

Flashbacks of holding his dead father in his arms shot like lightning through his head. His fists clenched as he paced the area.

As if Dusty knew what was going on, he bowed his head in grief and respect for the dead.

Dean tilted his head to the sky, letting the light of the moon wash over him.

He whispered, "I'll get him, Dad. I'll get him."

As tears threatened to sting his eyes, he reached into his pocket, pulled out the bottle of whiskey and took a sip. And poured a little out for his father, as he did every year on this day.

Anger washed over him, and a renewed determination to catch the bastard that killed his father had him seething. He inhaled deeply, took another swig and looked into the woods.

He'd get the son of a bitch.

As he turned to mount Dusty, something in his gut twisted. A foreboding of something to come.

CHAPTER 13

JULIE PULLED THE hood over her head and slipped out the back door. Goosebumps broke out over her skin as she jogged across the patio, careful to stay in the shadows and out of the light streaming from the windows. She held her breath—almost out of sight.

She exhaled as she slipped into the woods, covered by darkness.

Beams of light from the full moon shot through the trees, sparkling against the stubborn ice. She glanced over her shoulder before maneuvering through the thick brush, as she had done so many times already.

She knew the path like the back of her hand. Like the back of her lying, cheating, unfaithful hand.

Her pulse picked up when she hit the fields. Just about five more minutes. Just *five more minutes*. A small smile spread across her lips. She'd waited months to see him again. She'd fantasized about him, every single time her boring husband made love to her.

Made love. And that was exactly what it was. Her husband had made boring love to her when what she really wanted was to be *taken*. To be thrown onto the bed, her bra and panties ripped from her body in a wild, sexual frenzy. She wanted to feel the drip of sweat down her face as she was pounded, over and over again. She wanted to feel an earth-shattering orgasm. Was that really too much to ask?

The wind carried her perfume like an animal in heat. And she *was* in heat.

In the distance, the twinkling lights of the cabins came into view. Her pace picked up along with her heartbeat.

His light was on, waiting for her. Just like he always was.

She began to jog, despite the voice in her head telling her to calm down. Maybe play a little hard to get every once in a while, for Christ's sake.

As she drew closer, she hunkered down, doing her best to stay out of the view of the other cabins.

She saw his silhouette in the window.

Waiting for her.

The front door opened as she stepped onto the porch.

He smiled, she smiled back, and after a quick glance over her shoulder, she slipped inside.

The look in his eyes told her that he'd missed her too, and that she was in for one hell of an hour.

Without words, he took her in his arms and kissed her. A long, slow passionate kiss.

She pulled back. "I've missed you so much, Trevor."

"I've missed you, too. Here, let me take your coat."

That was the thing she liked most about him—that he never asked too many questions, or anything about her husband. Ever. He didn't care. Trevor was the type of guy who took things day by day, and didn't obsess about the future. He got to see her when she was in town; that was it. And that was just fine with him. He never called, texted, emailed or reached out in any way when she was home in Vermont. She ran the show.

It was the perfect affair.

He slid the coat off of her. "How are you doing?"

She looked down, her stomach knotted. "I... I'm still in shock, I think. I just... there's so much to do now."

"I'm so sorry." He clenched his jaw and glanced at the fire. "I just can't image who would do it. I mean, who would want Clint dead?"

She shook her head. "I don't know."

"How's Heidi?"

"The same. In shock, too."

"Did she see you leave?"

"No. Last time I saw her she was in the library, drinking wine and staring aimlessly out the window. With that damn, stinky dog next to her. God, I hate that dog."

"Dogs are good for protection." He reached forward and touched her cheek. "You need to watch yourself while you're in town."

She squeezed her eyebrows together. "What do you mean, watch myself? Do you think I'm in danger?"

"No. No, it's just... if something like that can happen to Clint, why can't it happen to anyone else? I mean, regardless, there's a murderer running around Berry Springs."

She swallowed the knot in her throat. She'd thought the same thing, too, but had pushed it away. It made her sick.

This is not what she wanted to talk about right now.

"I'll be careful."

He nodded and stepped closer, inches from her face.

Her heartbeat began to race as he took her face in his hands and kissed her, again.

She kissed back, hard. Melting into his strong arms.

With his lips still on her, he reached behind her and flicked the light switch. The room went dark except for the warm glow from the fireplace.

He slid off her cashmere sweater and unhooked her lace bra. The cold air swept over her bare breasts as she pulled off his shirt and inhaled the scent of his skin. The scent of her love affair, Trevor. The smell of a hardworking man.

He took her hand and guided her over to the bed. She sat, and watched him as he kicked off his boots and slid out of his jeans. She took a moment to look at his wide chest and bulging biceps and her body responded, wetting in preparation for what was to come.

The fire reflected in his dark eyes as he slipped out of his boxers.

She leaned back and rested on her elbows, gazing at his naked body in front of her, appreciating the comfortable rhythm they'd created after so many intimate affairs. Finally, he took off her pants and silk panties and tossed them across the room.

She felt the heat from the fireplace as she spread her knees for him. As she opened, she began to pulse with anticipation.

He kneeled down, pushed her knees farther apart and leaned forward. The warmth of his tongue against her skin shot a chill up her spine. He slowly licked her hips, her inner thighs, the crease of her leg and finally his tongue slid to her inner lips. Lightly at first, barely touching the skin, before sliding onto her clit. His hands gripped her thighs as he licked, squeezing her skin. He pressed in and took her greedily with his mouth, licking, sucking. She flushed wet with desire, her body vibrating with wild lust.

The heat of his mouth, the wetness of his tongue, the tingles he sent through her body—she couldn't take it. It had been too long.

Just as she was about to lose control, he pulled back and crawled over her. His rock-hard cock dangled over her abdomen.

She had to have him inside of her. *Right now.*

She grabbed his face, pulled him down and kissed him.

"Come on, Trevor. *Come on.*" She gripped his back.

He swept his tip down her stomach, against her opening, and then finally, he plunged inside of her.

She groaned and tipped her head back—her body closing in around him.

He slowly slid in and out, releasing a moan of pleasure in her ear as he began to pick up his pace.

With each push, the sexual frenzy inside of her built, the need to be *taken*—not *made love to*—intensifying. She bit her lip and thrust her hips forward, pushing him deeper inside her.

"Come on, Trevor."

He clenched his jaw and pushed deeper, faster; his breathing becoming heavier, a sheen of sweat breaking out over his skin.

"That's it, fuck me, Trevor, *fuck me.*"

He slammed himself into her, aggressively, over and over again, inching her whole body up farther in the bed with each thrust. She loved it.

He grabbed her wrists and pinned them down, squeezing so hard that she knew she'd have marks, like always.

Oh, God, she loved it when he did that.

He picked up the pace, faster, faster, taking her breath away as she wrapped her legs around him, pushing him in even deeper. Sweat beaded on her forehead.

His grip on her wrists tightened and she knew he was close.

"Oh, Trevor." The throbbing between her legs enhanced to a hot tingle, sending goosebumps across her body.

His voice low and husky, he said, "Are you close?"

Yes, oh, yes.

She nodded, her whole body tensing as he thrust himself into her. The sensation peaked and as she arched her back, he released, filling her with himself. She screamed, her orgasm pulsing through her body.

He collapsed onto her, his sweat-soaked skin sliding against hers.

Every muscle of her body melted into the mattress as she attempted to ease her racing heart with a few deep breaths.

He rolled off of her and took a deep breath. After a moment, he asked, "How long are you here for?"

She took a deep breath. "I guess until after the funeral."

A minute passed and she could feel a sudden shift in the room. A coldness that was beyond the temperature outside.

He pushed up on his elbows and looked over at her.

Her stomach sank. Call it a woman's instinct, but she knew she wasn't going to like what he was about to say.

"Look…" his voice was deep. And curt. "I think we should stop this."

Her eyes widened in shock. She sat up, and for a moment, she said nothing.

He continued, "With everything that's going on... it's just a lot."

What. The. Fuck!

It had literally been less than a minute since he had been inside her. She raised her eyebrows and looked over at him. "You couldn't have told me this ten minutes ago?"

He looked down.

She blew out a breath, laughed a laugh of disbelief, and pushed herself out of the bed. She was suddenly aware of how very naked she was. And embarrassed. She began hastily pulling on her clothes.

"I want to say I don't understand," she yanked her sweater over her head. "But honestly, I'm so damn embarrassed right now, I can't even look at you."

She couldn't get dressed fast enough, and for a fleeting moment she considered just walking outside the way she was and figuring the rest out later.

His silence was deafening as she pulled on her boots. What the fuck just happened? Why? They'd been having a passionate, perfect affair for years. *Years.* And she wasn't the only one that got off every time. Why stop now? All of a sudden?

Her head snapped up. She stared at him for a moment, narrowing her eyes. "There's someone else, isn't there?"

His gaze drifted to the floor, his shoulders hunching slightly.

There *was* someone else. She should have known. She should have known that their little affair wouldn't last. Of course it wouldn't—it was all one-sided. Her side. She had him whenever she wanted and then left him in the dust. Trevor was a good-looking, hard-working cowboy and she had no doubt that in the little hillbilly town of Berry Springs he was probably one of the most eligible bachelors.

Anger boiled in her veins, replacing the embarrassment, or perhaps, masking it.

"That's it, then." She shrugged nonchalantly and jerked the door open. "Was fun while it lasted."

She took one glance over her shoulder, sending a menacing glare in his direction before slamming the door shut.

Son of a bitch.

She grit her teeth and zipped up her coat.

As she stepped off the porch, rage bubbled up. The rage she'd inherited from her father. The rage that she kept pushed down her whole life. The rage that no medication seemed to be able to control.

What a *jerk!*

She shook her head and started across the field, her blood boiling. No one makes a joke out of Julie Davis.

No one.

CHAPTER 14

HEIDI LEANED HER head back, closed her eyes and took a deep breath, her shoulders releasing a tiny bit of tension. It had been thirty minutes since she'd heard her sister-in-law's nasally voice which made her shoulders shoot up to her ears. Thirty minutes of silence.

Julie made no secret of her dislike for Heidi. Everyone knew—Clint's father, the staff, her family, their friends. Everyone. And although she wasn't exactly sure what caused such disdain, she believed that it had something to do with another woman being in Clint's life. Part of her understood, based on their tough upbringing, but shit, did the woman have to make her life a living hell when she was around?

Passive aggressive was Julie's M.O. She always made comments like, *Oh, I see you switched around the furniture, oh, I see you cut your hair,* or, *I noticed more noisy wind chimes in the trees.*

Heidi didn't do well with passive aggressive. Hell, she'd spent hours trying to break almost every one of her clients from the nasty habit—just be direct and say what you mean, she'd tell them.

Her fingers gripped the wine glass in her hand. She felt completely out of control, overwhelmed, with no idea what the future held. And the feeling made her sick to her stomach.

She opened her eyes and looked out the windows, into the dark night.

Stop feeling sorry for yourself, Heidi, take action.

She took a sip of wine.

She could always move back to her hometown and reopen her clinic. Maybe live with her parents while she sorted things out. But living with her parents again? Hell, no. She loved her folks but the thought of moving back in with them made her feel desperate and needy, and she did not do desperate well.

For a split second, she regretted her decision to sign that damn prenup. But the truth was, she never wanted Clint for his money. Call her crazy, but she believed that his money was his, and hers was hers. She felt like she had no right to the Novak fortune, and that she'd get along just fine if anything ever happened. Of course, Clint was more than happy with that arrangement.

Now here she was, in the exact situation she never dreamed would happen when she signed the paper. Her husband of less than a year was dead, and she was a widow.

"Heidi?"

Startled, she nearly spilled her wine. She turned to see Jesse standing in the doorway.

"Yes?"

He walked into the room and handed her a stack of mail. "Here you go."

"Thank you." She took the handful of envelopes.

"You okay?"

"Yeah, thanks." She smiled and lifted her glass. "Wine helps."

"Always does." He turned. "I'm going to go check the horses."

"Sounds good."

As he left the room she looked through the stack of mail. She held up a letter addressed to her, forwarded from her office, with no return address. Even though the clinic was closed, she still received mail occasionally.

A chill slid up her spine as she carefully opened the envelope and unfolded the piece of notebook paper.

Heidi,

I miss you. You've been gone so long now and I think of you every day. As much as I try to forget about you, I can't. It seems you have burned yourself into my brain and I will never look at another woman the same way again. You're the only person who truly understands me and for that, I am forever indebted to you.

You are mine and I am yours, forever.

I can't wait to see you again,

Curtis

Her stomach sank. Curtis Eagan, her obsessed former

client. Her obsessed former client that apparently couldn't let go. Adding to the creepiness, the letter was handwritten in shaky cursive. This was the third letter he'd written her, and by far, the most disturbing. The others were accompanied by flowers or chocolates and simply told her that he was thinking of her, or that she was beautiful. Which was disconcerting enough, but this letter indicated a sick attachment. A possessiveness.

A very mentally-ill man.

Ding, ding.

She jumped—for the second time—at the sound of the doorbell. She glanced at the clock—nine-fifteen. Who would be visiting her now?

Apprehensive, she set down her wine glass and walked out of the library. She paused at the window, glanced outside and her heart skipped a beat. A patrol car.

Dean?

She quickly padded to the front door and opened it.

"Good evening, Mrs. Novak."

"Officer Hayes, good to see you, please, come in." Disappointment washed over her, but she forced a smile.

He stepped inside and she shut the door behind him.

"Is everything okay? What brings you by?"

He slid off his gloves. "Yes, everything's fine. Dean, I mean, Detective Walker thought it would be best if I stayed again, this evening. Keeping a watch out."

She exhaled. "That's a huge relief off my shoulders. Thank you. And please thank Detective Walker for me."

"Will do." He glanced past her toward the kitchen.

She smiled, knowing that he was looking for Eve. "Would you like some coffee? Tea?"

He nodded enthusiastically. "Yes, please, coffee would be great."

"Perfect, let's go."

As she led him to the kitchen her heart swelled, thinking of Dean. He'd found a way to protect her, to ensure her safety, without even being there.

"How are you holding up?"

"I'm doing okay; taking it minute by minute, hour by hour. Thanks for asking." She rounded the corner, into the kitchen. "Have there been any developments?"

"Not yet. But it's early yet, ma'am, don't worry."

She nodded and walked over to the coffee maker.

"So um, how's everyone doing?"

You mean, where's Eve.

"Everyone's holding up. I think Jesse and Eve are in for the night, down at the cabins," she looked at him from the corner of her eye and saw his shoulders slump. "And Trevor is staying tonight as well, I believe. Julie... I actually have no idea where Julie is. Probably up in her room."

* * *

Dean hesitated as he stopped at the bottom of his mother's driveway. Left, back to town? Or, right, to Heidi's? He glanced at the clock. It was already after nine. Was it too late to stop by?

He wanted speak to Julie as soon as possible and maybe catching her off guard would work in his favor. He also wanted to check on Hayes and make sure he was keeping his eye on the ball, and off of Eve's ass.

More than that, he wanted to see Heidi.

And that did it. He turned right and flicked on his high beams as he bumped down the long dirt road. His mother's house backed up to the Novak's land and it was only a few miles to the main house.

It had taken an arm and a leg to get Chief McCord to approve another night of security at the Novak Estate. Bottom line, Dean believed the shooter hadn't gone far, and that Heidi was still in danger. From who? No clue. Why? He had a few suspicions but nothing concrete, and there was nothing Chief McCord hated more than soft assumptions. But someone had killed Heidi's husband and come for her hours later—a fact that was pretty hard to ignore, and eventually, McCord caved.

He veered off the road, onto an even narrower dirt road, which was a shortcut that not many people knew about. His truck squeaked and groaned as it bounced over the deep ruts. Only hunters used this road, and not very often.

He sucked in a breath as the bottom of his truck drove over a hole and hit on a rock. *Dammit.*

He rounded a tight corner and the Novak's fields came into view. And something caught his eye.

He squinted and leaned forward.

What the hell?

Under the silver light of the full moon, a cloaked figure darted across the wide-open space. He quickly clicked off the headlights, slowed and grabbed his gun.

He glanced toward the cabins in the distance. Two

were dark, a dim light on in the third. If he recalled correctly, the cabin with the light on was Trevor's.

He looked back at the field.

Maybe it was one of the staff? The silhouette was definitely too small to be Jesse or Trevor; maybe it was Eve? No, it wouldn't be her, or any of the staff for that matter because Heidi had told him that they take horses or ATV's to and from the main house.

His pulse picked up.

He shoved the truck into park, turned off the engine and jumped out.

The freezing cold wind stung his face as he jogged around the truck. Careful to stay in the shadows, he darted across the road and with a seamless jump, scaled the barb-wire fence. He stayed low and jogged through the field, his eyes locked on the figure. He could either come up behind the person, or get ahead of them and flank them from the side.

He cut right, staying against the fence and pulled ahead. He slipped into the woods, paused behind a tree and listened.

The wind swept through the tall pine trees above him. A coyote howled in the distance.

Snick.

He looked in the direction of the sound and saw the figure maneuvering between the trees ahead of him.

He slowly crept forward, as quiet as a mouse, and edged closer.

Twenty feet away.

Ten feet.

He slid his finger over the trigger.

Suddenly, the moonbeams cut through the trees, illuminating the figure's face.

Julie.

He dropped his gun and jumped behind a tree. What the hell was she doing? Where was she going? Where had she been?

He watched her make her way out of the woods, crouch down and dart across the back lawn, and slip in through a back door.

Dean cocked an eyebrow.

Yes, this family was full of secrets.

CHAPTER 15

AS HE DROVE around to the front of the house, he scanned the area for anyone else that might be lurking in the woods. After seeing Julie's covert operation, he knew now, more than ever, that there was something going on with that woman. Did she murder her brother for the millions in his bank account? Possibly. And that's exactly what he needed to figure out.

He parked behind Hayes's patrol car and glanced inside as he passed by. No Hayes. Either he was doing a perimeter check, or was whipping up a four-course meal with Eve. He assumed the latter.

Although it was nine-thirty in the evening, the house was lit up, which was good because his mind was spinning with curiosities and questions about the Novak family, and it was his sole mission to have a sit down with Julie.

He noticed the front windows had been fixed and he wondered if either Jesse or Trevor had done it, or if she called someone from town.

As he stepped onto the porch, the front door opened.

He smiled and butterflies awoke inside him.

"Detective."

"Heidi."

She smiled back, holding his gaze. She was glad he'd stopped by; it was written all over her face. But there was something more in her eyes, in the look that she gave him—a warmth, desire. And it was that moment, for the first time, that he was one-hundred percent certain that she had been thinking of him just as much as he had been thinking about her. The undeniable chemistry between them was mutual. It was written all over her face. Tiny bubbles of excitement rushed through his veins—excitement that the woman who had consumed his entire being the last twenty-four hours, felt the same in return.

Her curly hair was down, falling softly over her shoulders and he imagined running his fingers through it, before grabbing her head and kissing her until her knees went weak.

"Please, come in."

He stepped inside and the faint smell of wood burning scented the air. His favorite smell. Just then, Gus barreled down the hall, his tail wagging wildly.

Dean tensed, still unsure about the animal. To his surprise, Gus tromped up to him and licked his arm. His new buddy.

Dean smiled and ruffled Gus's ears.

"Wow, y'all are best friends now."

"Appears that way."

Satisfied with the interaction, Gus sauntered back down the hall.

"How are you doing?"

"I'm making it. Is there anything new?"

Yes, your sister-in-law is my number one suspect. "We're looking at a few different angles right now."

"Anything you can share with me?"

"Not right now."

A fire crackled and popped in the den beside them.

She smoothed her sweater, seemingly nervous all of the sudden. Was it him, or something else?

"Would you like something to drink?"

"Sure."

As she led him through the house, he glanced around, looking for Julie.

"Supposed to have some more bad weather tomorrow."

"That's what I hear."

They stepped into the kitchen.

"I see Hayes made it. Have you seen him?"

She smirked. "He was chatting with Eve in the den a few minutes ago."

He shook his head. "Damn that boy. Where is he now?"

She laughed. "Don't be too hard on him, it's cute. I'm not sure where he is... let's see, I've got tea, soda, water, beer, wine, liquor, anything you want."

He hesitated for a moment, then thought, what the hell. "I'll take a beer. So where's Julie?"

Her face hardened at the mere mention of her sister-in-law. "Up in her room, I think."

Wrong, she's outside running covert missions in your woods.

He glanced outside. "How long is she staying with you?"

Heidi shrugged and handed him a beer. "Not sure... until after the funeral, I assume." She grabbed a beer for herself and his heart skipped a beat. A beautiful woman drinking a beer. Put a gun on her hip and he'd fall to his knees.

He leaned against the counter. "How long have she and her husband been married?"

Heidi blew out a breath and glanced up at the ceiling, searching her memory. "Oh gosh, a decade, maybe. They'd been married for a while when I met Clint."

"Happily?"

"I'm not sure, to be honest. I know they've had some... difficulties over the last few years." She leaned against the counter, across from him.

"Difficulties?"

"Rumors of affairs. Money problems. You know standard marital problems."

"Standard marital problems... you're certainly not making a case for marriage with that statement."

She laughed. "Have you ever been married?" She nodded toward his left hand. "I noticed you didn't have a ring on."

When did she notice that, he wondered?

"No, I've never taken the leap, to my mother's dismay."

"She's ready for grandkids?"

"I think that's the only reason she wants me to get married, to be honest."

Heidi smiled, and glanced away. "We'd just begun discussing children in our future."

He looked down, surprised by the fleeting moment of insecurity that crept into his head. For the first time, he wondered if Heidi missed her husband. Was she in love with him? He didn't feel that she was, but he could be wrong. He looked up and caught her eyeing him, studying him, as if she were reading his thoughts.

She continued, "But he wanted to wait for a while. Do you want children?"

"Absolutely." He smiled, "And not just to get my mom off my back about it."

She paused. "Why haven't you married?"

He took a sip of his beer, buying a moment. Pushing forty, he'd been asked that exact question more times than he could count, and the answer was always the same—he hadn't met the right one, like his father had promised he would, during the last conversation they'd ever had, moments before he was shot in the head.

"And then one day, you're going to meet one, and the second you see her it's going to be like a dagger piercing through your heart. You'll forget your name, all your pride and she'll be the only thing that matters to you... You'll know it in your gut, son. You'll know when she's the right one."

The same conversation that had run through his head countless times since he'd met Heidi Novak.

His gaze leveled on hers. "Just waiting to meet the right one."

Her eyes twinkled as she looked back at him. He could almost feel the electricity shooting between them. The kind of undeniable attraction that goes so much deeper than the surface; the kind that comes from the soul.

The kind that scares the shit out of him.

Maybe it was the beer, or the few shots of whiskey he'd had at his mother's house, but his thoughts clouded and the only thing clear to him was that the woman standing across from him had a place in his life, he was sure of it.

And he needed to keep her safe.

Her wide eyes were locked on his, a pleading for him to

say something. To say what was on his mind. She opened her mouth...

"Oh. Sorry. I didn't realize we had company." Julie paused in the doorway.

She was no longer in her long, black cloak, but he noticed that her hair was disheveled, which was a far cry from the woman he'd met earlier that looked like she'd spent two hours in front of the mirror. Her cheeks were flushed, her eyes hyper and alert.

Heidi cleared her throat. "Julie, you remember Detective Walker."

Dean noticed Julie's nerves as she looked at him. "Yes, good to see you, Detective."

"You, too."

"Have there been any developments?"

"No, but I was hoping you and I could sit down and chat this evening."

"Oh." Her eyes darted around the kitchen. "Sure, I guess."

"Great. Now?"

Reluctantly, she nodded. "Sure, come on." She turned and Dean glanced over his shoulder at Heidi before following Julie down the hall.

They stepped into the den, where Jesse had led him earlier—must be the unofficial interview room at the Novak house. And, ironically, she sat in the exact chair that Jesse had chosen right before he was questioned.

She sat, her back as straight as a rod, with her hands in her lap.

He watched her for a moment before saying, "I'm sorry about your brother."

She looked down. "Me, too."

Then, he began the delicate dance of questioning a suspect—who wasn't *officially* a suspect—without tipping them off that they were being questioned for murder.

He led with conversation. "I can't imagine how hard this must be for you, especially after recently losing your father."

"Yes, it's not even been a year."

"I understand Heidi has begun the funeral arrangements. Is there anything I can do to help?"

Something flashed in her eyes. "*I've* begun the funeral arrangements. Heidi is helping where she needs to, and I think we've got everything we need. Thanks."

There was no denying that this woman could not stand Heidi.

"You and Clint were pretty close?"

"Yes, very. As close as a brother and sister could be."

"How often did you two talk?"

"Every day." She took a deep breath. "Every single day."

"Julie, did Clint mention anything that might have led you to believe that he was in danger?"

Without hesitation, "No."

"No arguments with anyone recently?"

"No."

"Or, perhaps he mentioned someone who he might have been upset with?"

"No, not that I can recall."

"What about Heidi?"

"What about her?"

He stared at her for a second. "Anyone want her dead?"

Julie's eyes widened at his blunt choice of words. Good, he was throwing her off.

"Not that I'm aware of."

"Perhaps a jealous woman?"

A light chuckle. "Of Heidi? No, I doubt that."

"Maybe jealous of something Heidi had, like Clint."

"Are you suggesting that my brother was having an affair with another woman?"

He casually shrugged.

She shook her head. "No, I would have known. He would have told me, and besides, why would the woman kill Clint? Doesn't add up."

He inhaled and sat back. "That's a good point, it's not like the woman stood to gain anything from Clint's death."

Her eyes rounded. She caught the subtle insinuation like a lead balloon. She began picking her nails.

"When was the last time you spoke with Clint?"

"Yesterday afternoon."

"And what was the conversation about?"

She looked down. "He was returning my call."

"About what?"

Her hands twisted nervously in her lap. "About... a business deal."

"What business deal?"

"That's none of your business."

"Perhaps not, but knowing Clint's every movement in the days leading up to his death is my job. Where he went, who he spoke with and what those conversations were about might help uncover a stone that could lead to his killer."

She cocked an eyebrow and stared at him. Irritated

now, she blew out a breath, leaned forward and lowered her voice, as if she didn't want Heidi to hear. "I'd asked him to invest in my art shop, in Vermont."

"Business not good?"

"Unfortunately, no."

"What does your husband do?"

"He's an architect. *Self-employed*." Dean noticed the disapproval and disdain in her voice as she continued. "Business was good for a while, but then just dropped off."

"That must be tough on you."

"It is. My art shop was supposed to be a fun, side project. Now we're depending on it to pay the bills."

"What about your inheritance? Didn't you get anything from your father?"

She looked at him, her face hardened. "Not nearly as much as Clint. And what I got was just about enough to pay off half of our debt. It was gone the moment I got it."

"I'm sure Clint must have been more than happy to help you out and invest in your business, then. What did he say when you asked?"

"He said no."

"No?"

"That's right." She glanced out the doorway, toward the kitchen. "And I have no doubt that his wife persuaded that decision."

And there it was. Potentially, the biggest reason for the ice-cold hatred for Heidi.

"Why do you think that?"

"Because I can't think of any other reason why he wouldn't help me out."

Motive for Clint? Check. Motive for Heidi? Check.

He dove in. "Julie, can you recount your last forty-eight hours for me? Just for the record?"

Her raised her eyebrows. The nervous woman who'd sat down a few minutes ago was now defensive, curt, and ice-cold.

"I flew down two days ago to visit with a few local artists in Eureka, the next town over."

"For your art shop?"

"Yes."

"Did you see Clint while you were here?"

"No."

He cocked his head. "That surprises me, considering how close you two are."

"I was busy, and I'd planned to visit today, actually."

"Where did you stay?"

"At a little hotel downtown, The Pelican Inn."

"Nice place, I've been there a few times. Amazing restaurant."

"It's alright."

"Where else did you go?"

"I had dinner with an artist in the evening."

"Then what?"

"I went back to my hotel."

"Alone?"

Pause. "Yes."

"Alone the whole night?"

"Yes."

She shifted her weight, and began tapping her foot. She was about to walk out, he knew it.

"Julie, who stands to inherit Clint's money now that he's dead?"

She narrowed her eyes, her gaze piercing his. "I do, detective."

"Is that why you've opened offshore accounts in Switzerland?"

She clenched her jaw. "That's my damn business."

"Mine, too."

"What I do with my money is my business. It's my money to do with what I please, and I won't have my husband burning through it like he did my first inheritance." She pushed off the chair, her face flushed with emotion. "If you have any other questions for me, you can contact my lawyer."

He took one final shot in the dark.

"Will do. Hey, do you know if Trevor's available? I just drove by the cabins and noticed his light was still on... just didn't want to... interrupt anything."

Her eyes rounded with shock, then narrowed with rage as she stared back at him.

Bingo.

She turned on her heel and as she stomped out of the room, he called after her. "Hey, Julie? You might want to wipe that fresh mud off your boots."

There was a momentary break in her footsteps, before she continued stomping up the staircase.

Dean leaned back in the chair and exhaled. Julie Davis had just become the prime suspect in the murder of Clint Novak and attempted murder of Heidi Novak.

It was going to be a long night.

"Hey, detective."

He glanced over his shoulder as Hayes walked into the room.

The look in Dean's eye stopped him in his tracks. "What's going on?"

Dean stood, nodded outside and led Hayes out the front door. He closed it quietly behind him.

"Listen, I know you've got a hard-on for Eve but I need to you keep your eye on the ball, especially tonight."

"You think someone's coming for Heidi tonight?"

He wasn't sure, but every fiber of his being told him something was going to happen tonight.

"I'm going to bring the sister in for formal questioning."

Hayes's mouth gaped open. "The *sister*? Julie?"

Dean nodded. "She's got motive, for both Clint and Heidi, and has no alibi the night of the murder."

"Do you really think she killed her brother?"

The truth was, it seemed too obvious. *Way* too obvious. Either she was the dumbest murderer on the planet— which, hell, he'd seen before—or she didn't do it. But he couldn't ignore the fact that the motive was there, and either way, bringing Julie in for questioning would help to shed more light on the family, or, more light on her, if she did do it.

"That's what I've got to find out, and I need you to keep your head on a swivel. Keep your eye on Heidi, specifically."

"Yes, sir. Are you going to go get Julie now?"

Dean glanced into the dark woods. "I want to do a perimeter check first before I leave you guys for a few hours, to take her in."

"You're coming back? I thought I was on guard tonight."

Fuck, yeah, he was coming back. He wasn't going to let Heidi out of his sight until he arrested the son of a bitch that tried to kill her.

"Yeah, I'll be back." He turned and began walking down the steps.

"Dean?"

"Yeah?"

Hayes met him at the bottom of the steps. "Come here." He led Dean to his squad car and opened the door. After a moment shuffling through the console, Hayes handed him a revolver, zipped safely in an evidence bag.

"Eve's gun. The one you saw on her passenger seat."

Dean cocked an eyebrow. "Nice job, Hayes."

"Thanks. And, there's this..." Hayes handed him another plastic bag. "I found these in her fireplace."

Dean peered down at the charred pictures. In the center of the top photo was Julie's smiling face.

"You found these in Eve's fireplace?"

"Yeah. The rest are too burned to tell what they are. But they were recently burned, I could tell. Thought it was interesting. Why would she burn pictures of Julie?"

Dean nodded and his mind began to race. He tucked the pictures in his coat pocket. "I'll be back in an hour, maybe a bit longer."

"Okay."

As Hayes turned, Dean called out after him. "Hayes?"

"Yeah."

"Keep your eye on Heidi."

"Yes, sir."

CHAPTER 16

HEIDI LOOKED OUT the window for what seemed like the hundredth time since she'd watched Dean disappear around the side of the house.

It had been a little over an hour, and she knew something was up because Hayes had been lingering around her, not leaving her side since Dean had pulled him out on the front porch for what appeared to be an intense discussion. She'd had just about as much small talk with the young officer as she could take.

A line of worry ran across her forehead as she sipped her beer. What had happened during his conversation with Julie? Something had set her off; Heidi knew that because of the way Julie had stomped up the staircase and slammed her bedroom door, and she hadn't seen her since. Knowing Julie, she'd probably polished off a bottle of wine in her room and fell asleep.

A chill in the air spread goosebumps over her arms and she realized the fire had died down. The last twenty-four hours, she'd worked her butt off to keep the fire in the den going, not only for the additional heat but because something about a crackling fire put her at ease. And God knows she needed more *ease* than ever with her sister-in-law being there.

She glanced at the two measly twigs left in the stack of wood.

Dammit, time for a cold trip to the woodpile.

She turned, surprised that Hayes wasn't lingering in the doorway, pretending to be on his phone or something. When she didn't see him, she did a little celebratory dance in her head, grabbed her coat, slid on a pair of thick gloves and pulled a beanie over her head.

She glanced over her shoulder, looking for Hayes one more time, before walking out the front door.

The night was dark—pitch-black—and ice-cold. Dean's truck sat in the driveway, behind Hayes's patrol car. She scanned the yard before walking down the steps.

The woodpile was about ten yards from the main house and backed up to the woods. She zipped up her jacket and began walking across the yard, listening intently for Dean, or anyone that might be lurking in the shadows.

The night was quiet—eerily so.

A chill ran up her spine.

She glanced over her shoulder, actually hoping to see Hayes, before picking up her pace. Nerves tickled her stomach. She shouldn't have come outside alone, or, she should have told Hayes where she was going, at the very least.

The wood pile came into view and she had to refrain from jogging to it. She was creeped out and wanted to get back in the house STAT.

She tightened her gloves as she stepped up to the pile and grabbed the first log she could reach. Her gaze lifted to the dark woods just a few feet in front of her, and suddenly she got an unnerving feeling, like she was being watched.

Her heart pounded as she hastily grabbed another log, sending a few pieces of wood tumbling behind the stack.

"*Dammit.*"

As she stepped around the side of the woodpile, her toe caught a tree root and she stumbled to the ground, sending the logs flying out of her arms and into the darkness.

Her breath was knocked out of her as she hit the ground.

She released a low groan and blinked the fuzziness from her eyes. Pain shot through her ankle as she rolled over.

Like a jolt of electricity, terror shocked her system. Her pulse skyrocketed as she scrambled backward... away from the body sprawled out in front of her.

"Oh, my God."

Her heart hammered in her chest as she crawled forward.

"Julie?" Panic seized her. "*Julie?!*"

Dressed in a long, black trench coat, her sister-in-law lay on her side, her head twisted, her face buried in the ground.

She grabbed Julie's arm and shook it. "*Julie?*"

Silence.

Her voice pitched. "*Julie?*"

She slowly rolled the body over and as Julie's head lobbed clumsily to the side, a single stream of blood trickled from the bullet hole in the middle of her forehead.

Her scream vibrated through the air as she fell backward. The world spun around her.

She had to get the hell out of there.

She pushed off the ground, turned and lunged directly into Dean's arms.

His eyes were wild with panic. "Are you okay?"

She shook her head from side to side, unable to form a sentence.

He looked past her, then back to her. "*Heidi, are you okay? Are you hurt?*"

"No, I'm fine," she whispered. "It's Julie."

He kept a firm hold on her and reached for his cell phone just as Hayes burst through the front door.

"*Hayes, over here!*"

Hayes ran across the lawn, pulling his Glock from his belt.

"Get Heidi inside."

Hayes gaped down at Julie's body.

"*Hayes, now!*"

Hayes grabbed Heidi, but before Dean let go, he grabbed her face. "I'll be right here. Go inside, I'll be there in just a second. You're okay, you're going to be okay."

Breathless, she nodded as Hayes grabbed her by the shoulders and pulled her away.

* * *

Dean pulled his gun, turned on his heel and scanned the woods while Hayes guided Heidi back inside. Once she was safely behind closed doors, he turned and kneeled down.

Julie's lifeless eyes stared up at him, a look of distress frozen on her flushed face.

She was fresh. He guessed within the last twenty minutes.

He looked at the single bullet hole between her eyes

and clenched his jaw. Carefully, he turned her head—her blonde hair was matted with blood.

The bullet had gone through her skull.

Adrenaline surged him to his feet and he turned around, ready to fight. He listened for any noise, any movement, but the night was quiet, except for the whistle of the cold wind through the trees.

He looked down at the body, imagining the moments before her death. What was she doing outside, again? Why behind the woodpile? Was she dragged behind the pile? Where was the shooter? Hiding in the woods, no doubt about that.

Based on the way her body laid on the ground, Dean determined the shooter must've stood right where he was standing. But her head was whipped to the side, so he must have shot her at an angle. Did she see him? Even know he was there?

He grabbed his flashlight and surveyed the ground, and the woods. No tracks, no broken branches, twigs or signs that anyone had been through recently.

Sirens wailed in the distance and Dean took a step away from the body.

He glanced up at the house and his chest squeezed. What if it had been Heidi? What if she'd been killed instead of Julie? Did the killer mistake Julie for Heidi? The thought made his stomach churn, and that churn quickly turned into fire.

Lights bounced off the trees as a patrol car sped up the driveway.

Dean walked to the driveway as the car stopped behind

his truck. The door swung open as more headlights and sirens sounded in the distance.

"What the fuck's going on?" Willard zipped up his coat and briskly walked up the driveway.

"Another body."

An ambulance parked behind Willard's car.

"You're shitting me. Where?"

"Behind the woodpile. Clint's sister."

Willard's eyebrows shot up. "Holy shit."

"Yeah." Dean glanced behind Willard to the medic, scurrying up the driveway. "Be right back."

He crossed the driveway. "Dr. Buckley…"

"Hey, Dean. What we got?"

"Woman, shot between the eyes. But I want you to check on Heidi Novak first. She's inside. In shock."

He nodded. "Will do."

"Thanks."

Dean turned toward the woodpile where bursts of light flashed through the darkness. Willard had begun taking pictures of the scene.

He walked over.

Willard looked up and shook his head. "There goes our prime suspect."

Dean glanced toward the field. "I've got to go have a chat with someone."

Willard cocked an eyebrow. "Yeah? Got someone in mind already?"

"We'll see. Are you good here for a little while?"

"Yeah, I'll get these pictures done and then we'll bag her up and take her in."

Dean nodded. "I might need you in a second. Keep

your phone on. And block off this area. Don't let anyone walk all over the scene."

"You got it. Hayes inside?"

"Yeah." He turned and started toward his truck, but hesitated. He wanted to check on Heidi and knew he wouldn't have a clear head until he knew she was okay. As he stepped onto the porch, Dr. Buckley pushed through the front door.

"How is she?"

"Fine. Shaken up, but fine. Her heart rate is sky high, but I've got her relaxing. She'll be alright after some rest. She needs to relax, she's been through too much in the last two days."

"Okay, thank you."

"Not a problem. She's a nice woman; beautiful, too. Wonder why something like this happens to someone like that."

Dean glanced through the window. He had no answer for that.

"I'll swing back in before I leave." The doctor hesitated, and frowned. "Dean, two murders in two days... does not make me feel warm and fuzzy inside."

"I'll get him. I'll get him soon."

"Please do."

Dean pushed through the front door and walked into the house. He glanced in the den, where Heidi was sitting in a chair, staring blankly into the fire and clutching a glass of wine. Hayes sat on the couch across from her and stood up the moment he saw Dean.

He waited in the hallway to talk to Hayes before walking into the room.

"How is she?"

"Okay. Better. I got her some wine."

"Good. Buckley is going to check on her again before he leaves."

"I saw Willard pull up."

"He's photographing the scene." Dean looked past Hayes, at Heidi. "Let me talk with her for a second, okay?"

Hayes nodded. "I'll go talk to Willard, will be back in a sec."

"Sounds good."

As Dean walked into the den, Heidi turned and locked eyes with him.

His heart skipped a beat.

She inhaled and seemed to soften when she saw him. "Hi."

He kneeled down at her feet and put his hand on her knee. "Are you okay?"

She nodded, and put her hand over his. The fire popped and hissed behind them and for a moment, they just stared at each other. They looked at each other with the weight of events that had unfolded, and with understanding and acknowledgment of what was happening between them. He saw it in her eyes. No words needed to be spoken. They had a connection, deeper than he'd ever felt. And although they barely knew each other, they knew enough.

"Your heart rate is high."

"I heard."

He nodded toward the wine. "Can I get you some more? Or maybe tea?"

"No, thank you." Tears filled her eyes. "Dean. Who…"

A fresh wave of anger coursed through him. Seeing the

pain on her face made him absolutely crazy. He gripped her knee and leaned forward. "I'll get him, Heidi, I'll get him. I need you not to worry, okay?"

A tear ran down her cheek and she nodded.

He reached up, wiped the tear, then stood and looked down at her. He softly swept the hair from her face.

"You're going to be okay. I'm going to make sure of that."

He glanced out the window and saw Hayes walking onto the porch.

"I've got to go check some things out." He bent over and whispered in her ear. "I'll be back."

She reached up and grabbed his hand. "Dean, be careful."

He nodded, kissed her softly on the forehead, then met Hayes at the front door.

"Keep an eye on her."

"Yes, sir."

CHAPTER 17

SMOKE ROLLED FROM the chimney as Dean stepped up to the front door of the cabin. The low light of a single lamp glowed from behind the curtains, which were pulled tightly shut. He glanced at his watch before knocking—almost eleven-thirty.

The moment he knocked, he saw a shadow move briskly across the room. Then, nothing.

Another knock.

Finally, the door opened.

"Good evening, Trevor." Dean looked him over. Trevor showed no signs of having been asleep and was wearing flannel pants and an NRA sweatshirt. He quickly glanced at the floor, looking for muddy boots, or prints, or anything that might have indicated that Trevor had been out in the woods this evening.

Trevor's eyebrows raised with surprise. "Detective, what's going on?"

"May I come in?"

Pause. "Sure."

Trevor opened the door and Dean stepped inside. The

faint smell of a microwave dinner lingered in the air—enchiladas if he had to guess. He looked around—the television was on, a beer sat on the table in front of the couch.

The bed was a mess.

The house was sparsely decorated, which made it easy for him to take a quick inventory.

His gaze landed on a small gun chest in the corner of the room. Hunting rifles, knives and a pistol sitting on top. Loaded pistols, ready for action, sit on top of cabinets, not in them.

"Cozy place."

"Thanks." Trevor stood in front of the small kitchen table and crossed his arms over his chest, obviously wanting Dean to get to the point of the late-night visit.

Dean casually unzipped his jacket, flashing the Glock on his hip. Not that he needed to, the sheer size and mass of Dean was enough to intimidate any man in town. Or, the tri-state area for that matter.

"You don't usually stay here, do you?"

"No, I have an apartment in town."

"Why'd you choose to stay tonight?"

"Considering everything that's gone on the last few days, I wanted to stay close."

"In case Heidi or Julie needed you?"

Something in his dark eyes flickered. "Yeah."

"That's nice of you." Dean glanced at the beer on the coffee table. "What have you been up to this evening?"

Trevor's brow furrowed. "Not much. Was just about to go to bed."

"How about before then?"

Pause. "After putting the horses up for the evening, I came here."

"Straight here?"

"Yep." His tone was sharp now; he was starting to get annoyed—a common emotion at the Novak Estate.

"What time?"

"About seven-thirty."

"Did you go anywhere after that?"

"Nope."

A moment of silence ticked by as Dean watched him.

"Any company this evening, Trevor?"

Trevor looked down for a moment, then quickly looked back up. "Why are you asking me these questions, detective?"

"Just being thorough; I'm sure you understand that. I spoke with Julie an hour or so ago." Dean stared at him for a moment. "Just making my rounds, you know"

Trevor took a deep breath and dropped his arms. "So she told you."

No, but you just did.

Dean slowly nodded, but kept his mouth shut hoping Trevor would elaborate.

He did. "Look... it's gone on for a while. I'm not proud of it." He began pacing and ran his fingers through his graying hair. "And I recently met someone. So I ended it with her; with Julie."

"Tonight?"

Trevor nodded.

"How'd she take it?"

Trevor laughed. "'Bout as I expected."

"What time was this?"

"Around nine o'clock."

"And then what happened?"

"She left. Pissed as shit."

"And that was it?"

"No." He blew out a breath. "She texted me, 'bout forty-five minutes ago and wanted to talk, again."

"Did you respond?"

"Yes, I said she could come back by whenever. Probably shouldn't have, but..." he shrugged.

"And then what did you do?"

"Ate dinner and drank some beer, waiting on her."

"That's it?"

Trevor raised his eyebrows. "I took a piss and a shower, too, detective. What the hell's going on?"

"What's going on is that I just found Julie with a bullet to the head."

Dean carefully watched Trevor as his mouth gaped open, his eyes growing to the size of golf balls.

"Trevor, I'm going to need to bring you in for formal questioning."

"*What?* Are you serious?"

"I am. You can either do it calmly now, or I'll bring the team down, we'll handcuff you and take you in the back of a squad car."

The blood drained from Trevor's face. Eventually, he raised his hands as if to surrender. "Alright, alright."

"Good." Dean reached into his pocket and pulled out his cell phone. Keeping his gaze on Trevor, he called Willard.

Moments later, a patrol car pulled in front of the cabin.

"Let's go." Dean stepped aside and motioned Trevor to the front door.

Willard stood outside with the backseat door open. After guiding Trevor into the patrol car, he shut the door and turned to Dean.

"What'd you have on him?"

"A lengthy affair with Julie that he just ended two hours ago, and she was on her way to meet him."

Willard nodded. "That'll do it."

"Take him to the station, keep him as long as you can. I'm going to talk with Eve and Jesse as well. Hayes still with Heidi?"

"Yep."

"Good. Alright. We'll talk soon."

"You got it."

As Willard drove down the driveway, Dean walked back into Trevor's cabin, flicked on a light, and kneeled down in front of the threshold. Not a speck of dirt; fresh, at least. He looked at the doormat, nothing. Trevor's boots lay in a perfect line next to the door. He carefully picked them up and turned them over. Clean as a whistle.

He stood and did a lap around the cabin, steering clear of the bed sheets. Beer, milk, lunch meat and hotdogs in the fridge, frozen dinners in the freezer. Dishes piled in the sink. A stack of newspapers on the kitchen table. Nothing under the bed. He poked through the trash—beer cans, wrappers, empty boxes, banana peels. No messages on the answering machine, no computer to search through. Nothing stood out other than the fact that Trevor was a very, very simple man.

Before leaving, he slid on a pair of latex gloves, pulled the pistol from the top of the gun cabinet and slid it into an evidence bag, and into his jacket.

He stepped outside, closing the door behind him.

"Detective?" Jesse closed his front door and stepped outside. "What's going on?"

Just then, a light flicked on in Eve's cabin and her front door opened. Wearing flannel pajamas and a pink robe, her eyes rounded with concern. "Detective? Is everything okay?"

Dean looked from Jesse, to Eve. "I was hoping to speak with you both this evening."

Jesse stepped off his porch and walked the few short steps to Eve's cabin. "What's going on?"

Dean turned to Eve. "Mind if I come inside?"

"No, not at all." She stepped aside and opened the door widely.

Dean quickly scanned the room as Jesse walked in after him.

Eve stood frozen, staring at him, waiting for him to explain the purpose of the visit. Concerned, too, Jesse crossed his arms over his chest and leaned against the couch.

"Eve, can you recount your evening for me?"

She nodded, the messy, blonde bun bobbing on top of her head. "Uh, sure, after making dinner for Heidi and Julie, I came home, made myself dinner, had a glass of wine, watched television, spoke with my sister and then went to bed. That's about it."

"What time was this?"

"I got home about eight, and was asleep by nine-thirty or so."

He'd have Jonas hack into her phone records and verify the time she spoke with her sister.

"Did you see anyone outside?"

"No, but I had the curtains drawn."

He turned to Jesse. "What about you?"

"I ran some errands in town, got back around seven, came by here, then checked on Heidi and that's about it."

"Did you see anyone? In the woods, by the house?"

"No, no, I don't think so."

"What about cars parked on the side of the road?"

He shook his head.

"Did you go out after you got back?"

"No, stayed in. Too damn cold outside. What's going on detective?"

He paused for a moment. "Julie has been murdered."

Eve gasped, and in perfect unison, she and Jesse said, "*What?*"

Dean watched them closely.

Jesse's fists clenched as he pushed off the couch. "Is Heidi okay?"

"Yes."

Jesse began pacing, his face and neck flushing with emotion. "First Clint, now Julie?"

"Oh, my God, who…" Eve covered her mouth, her eyes filling with tears.

"Do you have any suspects?"

"We're investigating several angles."

"Where's Trevor?"

Dean paused. "How well do you both know Trevor?"

Jesse cocked an eyebrow. "Pretty damn good." Pause. "You don't think…" His voice trailed off.

"Were he and Julie friends?"

Jesse cut a glance at Eve, which told Dean everything he needed to know.

"They were friends."

Dean looked at Eve. "More than friends?"

She slowly nodded.

"Okay. Did he have any other women in his life?"

"He'd been talking about someone he'd met at Frank's bar, a few weeks ago."

"Got a name?"

Jesse shook his head. "No, he didn't say much about her."

"Jesse, can I speak with Eve alone?"

Jesse glanced at Eve, not moving a muscle. He was protective of her, no doubt about that.

Eve gave Jesse a slight nod—if Dean wouldn't have been looking for it, he would've missed it.

"Okay, I'll just be next door."

"Thanks, Jesse."

As Jesse pulled the door shut behind him, Eve sank in the kitchen chair, her face as pale as a ghost.

"Eve, what was your relationship like with Julie?"

"Um, good, I guess. We really weren't close. She didn't talk to us much, to be honest."

"Except for Trevor."

"Right."

"Did you like her?"

She hesitated. "Yes."

"Why the pause?"

"She... she just wasn't very nice."

"Elaborate."

"Rude, self-centered. She was rude to me and Jesse. Treated us like *staff*, if you know what I mean."

"That must be hurtful."

Eve nodded.

Dean stared at her, letting the silence drag out.

"Anyway, she and I really didn't have a relationship. She just ordered me around, and that was it."

"Why would you burn pictures of her?"

Eve's head shot up. "What?"

"Why would you burn pictures of her?"

"How did you know..." She glanced at the fireplace, her eyes rounding as she put the pieces of the puzzle together. "I see." She shook her head. "Hayes is good at his job, isn't he?"

No response.

She blew out a breath. "The pictures weren't of Julie. They were of Earl, Julie and Clint's dad. Julie was in them, but they were of him." She stood and began pacing. "He and I developed a friendship over the last year."

"Just a friendship?"

Her pale face flushed. "Maybe a little more. He kissed me once. That's it, I promise."

He strongly doubted that, and the thought of an older man taking advantage of his young, cute employee made him want to punch a hole through Earl's head.

"Why burn his picture?"

She began nervously rubbing her hands together. "Because no one knew; it was our secret, and then when Clint was killed, I just... freaked out and burned them."

As he watched Eve nervously tick like a miniature poodle, it was hard to imagine her shooting Clint or Julie between the eyes.

But he'd confirm that when he got his hands on her revolver.

CHAPTER 18

I T WAS FIVE in the morning by the time everyone left the Novak Estate. Willard had come back after dropping Trevor off at the station and helped Dean survey the area for any evidence or clues to Julie's murder. According to Hayes, Heidi had finally fallen asleep around three in the morning, and after Dean personally checked on her, he left Hayes in the kitchen with Eve to make breakfast, while he went home for a quick shower before going into the station.

Not surprisingly, Trevor was none too happy to have been left in the station overnight, and was even more pissed when Dean left him hanging in the morning, again.

Dean was running purely on caffeine and adrenaline by the time he stepped into his office at seven-thirty in the morning.

He'd just sat in his chair when Chief McCord appeared in the doorway.

"Your prisoner is one pissed off citizen."

Dean appreciated the fact that McCord was a no-bullshit, no small-talk kind of guy who got straight to the point, but shit, could he just have a second to breathe?

Dean grunted and turned on his computer.

"The clock's ticking. I'm shocked he hasn't called a lawyer yet."

"I don't think he's the type to call one."

"Even country boys know their rights, Dean. And you can't hold him for more than twenty-four hours."

"He'll get released as soon as I get his gun checked out."

"What gun?"

"The loaded gun I found on top of his gun cabinet."

"Wesley have it already?"

Dean leaned back in his chair, irritation written all over his face. "I'll call him as soon as you give me a second to do it."

McCord cocked an eyebrow. "Alright, then, get it done and I want a full report. Lanie from NAR news has already called me. *Already*."

He shook his head and looked at his computer screen. *Dammit.* "Will do, sir."

"And one more thing. We're all tapped out on Mrs. Novak's personal security."

Dean looked at the chief. "She needs security, McCord. Someone killed her husband, tried to kill her, and just killed her sister-in-law."

"Well, she'll have to find it in the form of friends or a sawed-off shotgun. Hayes is called off at the end of the day, today. We can't afford it, Dean."

Dean's fists clenched under his desk. "McCord..."

The chief turned, walked away and Dean took a deep breath. He'd been expecting that, and honestly, he was surprised that McCord had approved the personal security in the first place.

But one thing was for certain, Heidi wasn't going to be left alone until he found his killer, so he'd just have to figure something out. For now, she was safe and he had other business to take care of.

He opened his email—sixty-seven unread emails. Son of a bitch. As he scrolled through, Jameson knocked on his office door.

"Mornin', Walker."

"Morning."

"Hell of an evening last night, huh?"

Dean let out a snort as Jameson took a seat across from him.

"McCord filled me in—Clint's sister, can't believe it. Shot between the eyes, right?"

"Yep."

"Bullet still in the head?"

"Nope, went through. Didn't find it."

Jameson shook his head. "Your suspect is pissed as shit, and on his second gallon of coffee, which is only making him more pissed. You need me to take this thing over?"

"No, no, I've got it." His stomach clenched.

"Okay man, just let me know what you need, alright?"

Dean nodded.

Jameson tossed a piece of paper on his desk. "Got the vehicle scan back from Clint's truck."

"Already?"

"Yep, came through last night."

"Wow, that was fast." In his experience, speed of reports wasn't necessarily a good thing. It either meant that the case was top priority, which was always good, or that nothing was found, which was the worst case scenario. He was hoping for the former.

"Good news first, the tread on Clint's tires match the tracks we found on the cliff."

"That's something."

"Yep, and the blood on the seat is Clint's."

"Okay, so what's the bad news?"

"Nothing else was found. No DNA from a passenger, or the killer or whoever, and no fingerprints, other than Clint's."

Dean leaned back in his chair and paused for a moment, thinking through the multiple scenarios in his head. "So we now know, one-hundred percent that Clint was shot in his truck, in the driver's seat. Presumably on the cliff, considering that's where the body was found and the tracks match."

"Right."

"So our perp, who presumably had on a pair of gloves, kicked Clint out of the truck, jumped in the driver's seat and drove his truck into the river."

"And opened the doors in an attempt to flood it and get rid of any evidence he could have left."

"Exactly."

"Clint must've known whoever killed him."

Dean chewed on his lip for a moment before picking up the phone.

"Jessica here."

"Morning, sunshine." He put the phone on speaker.

"*Dammit,* Dean it's too early to call me, asking for shit."

Jameson leaned into the speaker. "Good morning, princess, don't act like you're busy."

"Jameson, what the hell are you doing awake? I don't need both you guys hounding me for shit."

Dean chuckled. "How do you know I'm not just calling to say hi?"

"Because I'm not a six-foot blonde with big tits and a tight ass."

He laughed out loud. "Alright, I'm calling to see what you've got on our boy Clint so far."

"I plan to finish up the autopsy today, you'll get the report."

"What have you found out so far?"

"Besides the fact that you're annoying?"

Jameson grinned.

"Can you just tell me if he had any defense wounds?"

She blew out a breath of annoyance. "Clint was covered head to toe in bruises, scratches and cuts, but all were post-mortem."

"You're sure?"

"Fuck you."

He smirked, and continued. "No DNA under his nails or anything at all?"

"Nope. The bruises and shit happened after he was shot."

"From being dumped out of the truck and rolling off the cliff."

"That would be my assumption."

"What about the bullet in his head? Already pulled that out?"

"Yep, and *yes*, I plan to give it to Wesley to look over before we send it down to the state crime lab."

"Today?"

"Yeah, sometime today."

"Perfect, thanks Jess."

"Now leave me alone."

"Will do, sweetheart."

She laughed and clicked off the phone.

Jameson's cell phone beeped and he stood. "No defensive wounds mean, more than likely, Clint knew his killer and willingly let him into the truck. At least that helps narrow it down. I gotta go make a call. Let me know if you need anything else."

In deep thought, Dean nodded as Jameson walked out of his office.

He exhaled and picked up the phone.

"Wesley here."

"Wesley, it's Dean."

"Speak of the devil, I was just about to call you... was going to wait until the sun came up, at least."

Dean glanced out the window at the golden rays of sunlight beginning to wash over Summit Mountain.

"Sun's up."

"Gun's up."

"I think you mean, sun's out, gun's out."

"Nope. Sun's up, gun's up."

Dean smirked and shook his head. Wesley was always alert and on point, no matter what time of day it was.

"I've got a gun I need you to look at. Swipe for gunpowder; let me know how long ago it had been shot, and if it matches that casing I dropped off to you earlier. Also, a revolver. But look at the pistol first."

"That's why I was about to call you. I looked at that casing last night—it belongs to a forty-five semi-automatic handgun."

"Okay, what—

"I'm not done—you got lucky on this one. The firing pin markings on the primer indicates a blocking system."

"What the hell is a blocking system?"

"It's basically internal levers and a plunger that blocks the pin from moving until the trigger is pressed—think of it as an additional safety feature."

"Okay, so how many guns have that?"

"Quite a few, but on a hunch, I compared the casing to one of my guns with a block, and the markings were very similar."

"How similar?"

"Very. My gut tells me you're looking for a Colt 1911."

Dean raised his eyebrows. He never expected to get information that specific. "Damn, Wesley, I owe you."

"Yep."

"What time do you want me to drop the guns off?"

"I'm in town. I'll just swing by."

"Perfect, see you soon."

Click.

Dean glanced up at a knock at the door.

"Hey, Dean."

"Jonas. You're here early."

"Just mixing things up. Heard about the sister." He cocked his head. "Have you slept? You look like shit."

"Thanks."

"Any suspects?"

"Yeah, he's hanging out in the interview room."

"I wondered who the hell that was. Looks pissed."

"Well, then, I guess I should just leave him there until he cools off, right?"

Jonas grinned and laid a stack of papers on Dean's desk. "Got the soil analysis back."

"From the tire tracks on the cliff, and footprint on Heidi's porch?"

"Yep," he cocked an eyebrow, "Both contain a fertilizer. The *same kind* of fertilizer."

Dean sat up, a surge of energy rushed through him. This was the first official information linking both Clint's shooter to Heidi's shooter.

"Tell me it's more than shit, Jonas."

"Yes. Well, it's bio-fertilizer, specifically. Which is an expensive organic fertilizer. And only one place in town sells it."

"Tad's?"

"Yep."

A tingle of excitement ran up his spine. "Get me all the names of people who've bought it recently and pull the security camera footage."

"That's number one on my to-do list today, boss."

"Thanks."

As Jonas turned, Dean called out after him.

"Jonas?"

"Yeah?"

"I need you to pull phone records for Julie Davis, and our impatient guest. Check the communication for last night."

"Want me to do that now, or fertilizer first?"

"Shit first."

"You got it." Jonas started to walk out, but then turned back around. "Bad weather's coming today. *Really bad.*"

Dean frowned. He knew more winter weather was on its way but he hadn't exactly had a chance to check the weather.

"Define *really bad?*"

"Two inches of ice and over a foot of snow on top of it."

He cringed. That was definitely worse than the last report he'd heard.

"*Son of a bitch.*"

"Yeah, supposed to begin early this afternoon."

Dean took a deep breath. He'd better get moving, then.

***

Heidi hung up the phone, leaned back in her chair and glanced out the window. It was a cold, bleak day. Thick, gray clouds darkened the west, promising a sleet and snow storm to come. She glanced at the clock—almost five-thirty in the evening. She'd just got off a long call with the funeral director and was officially beat.

It had been another hell of a day.

She'd slept until after eight, which was extremely late for her, but not considering that she hadn't gone to bed until three in the morning. After dragging herself out of bed and greeting Hayes downstairs, she'd spent the day on and off the phone with Julie's husband and busying herself with funeral arrangements; choosing pictures, flowers, and poems, and writing the obituaries, for both Clint and his sister.

It would be a double funeral.

Her stomach churned as she stood and walked downstairs.

The front door opened.

"Hey."

She smiled as Hayes stepped inside and wiped his boots on the doormat.

He smiled. "Hey, how are you?"

"Good. Any colder outside?"

He pulled off his gloves and nodded. "The front is definitely moving in."

As if on cue, sleet began to tinkle against the windows.

"And there it is. Were you making rounds?"

"Just did a full perimeter check. No murderers lurking in the shadows."

She laughed softly. "That's the best news I've heard all day. Want some coffee?"

"Sounds great, thanks."

She led him to the kitchen. "Any word on when to expect Trevor home?"

"We can't hold him for more than twenty-four hours, which would be about midnight tonight."

She shook her head. "I just can't believe he'd do it, Hayes."

"Did you know they were having an affair? Him and Julie?"

She walked to the coffee maker and pulled the coffee from the jar. "No, I honestly didn't. But... it doesn't really surprise me. I'd picked up on the fact that she and her husband weren't exactly in love." She added water and pressed the brew button. "Regardless, I can't imagine Trevor killing her."

"We've got to make certain."

"I understand." She turned and walked to the window. The sleet had already begun to pick up. "Does this mean that you think he could have killed Clint as well?"

Hayes hesitated. "Detective Walker will have to answer that for you."

She nodded. "Where is he?"

"Last I heard, at the office. He's got a ton to do, and even more red tape to cross now that we have two victims."

Will he come by this evening? She wanted to ask, but didn't. "Were Eve and Jesse down at the cabins?"

"Jesse was chopping firewood and Eve's light was on in her cabin."

"You didn't check on her?"

"No, ma'am."

She poured two cups of coffee, handing him one. "Why not?"

"Well... she might not be too happy with me."

"Why?"

Heidi already knew about Hayes taking the pictures from the fireplace and swiping Eve's revolver, *and* about the "single kiss" between Eve and Heidi's father-in-law. Eve had come to the house to check on Heidi late last night, after the Julie incident, and after two glasses of wine, Eve spilled her guts to Heidi and cried about Hayes's *betrayal*, as she called it. By the end of the conversation, it was evident that Eve had real feelings for Hayes and although Heidi understood how Eve felt slighted by the officer, she wanted to get a read on Hayes's interpretation of the situation.

He sipped the coffee. "It's good, thanks."

"You're welcome. Now, why wouldn't our Eve be happy with you?"

He hesitated, then looked up, with defiance in his eyes. "It's my job to keep you safe, Mrs. Novak, and assist Dean in any way that I can."

She cocked her head. "Okay…"

"Which means, I'm obligated to look at everyone as a suspect and act accordingly."

"I see. So you had to look into Eve, making her feel like shit in the process? Actually, worse than shit because she has feelings for you, Hayes. I'm sure she feels bamboozled by you now… like you were using her." She sipped her coffee, watching him over the rim.

His eyes rounded. "You really think she has feelings for me?"

"I do."

He glanced out the window, letting this new, exciting information sink in.

"You probably should apologize."

His eyebrows shot up. "*Apologize?*"

"Uh-huh." She nodded.

He began pacing. "You want me to apologize for doing my job?" He took a quick, deep breath and shook his head. "No, no, ma'am. I shouldn't have to apologize. I was just doing my damn job."

She almost laughed at his sudden rush of emotions. Yep, this guy definitely had real feelings for Eve.

She shrugged. "Suit yourself. I'm sure you'll find another girl as sweet, smart and pretty as Eve. And by the way, I think Jesse's got the hots for her, too. Won't be too long before he makes a move."

Hayes's face dropped and he glanced out the window, toward the cabins.

Heidi laughed. "Go tell her you're sorry, you idiot."

He turned to Heidi and a small smile spread over his lips. "Okay."

"Good. Smart boy."

He set his coffee cup on the table. "I'll be right back."

"No hurry."

Heidi watched Hayes practically run out of the front door, and her heart swelled. He was like a teenager dealing with his first rush of love.

She thought of Dean and how he made her feel like that, too. He gave her butterflies; or hell, a flock of hummingbirds was more like it. He made her feel giddy, just like a school girl in love. Over the last few days, she realized she'd never felt that from Clint. Over the last few days, she couldn't put her finger on why she'd married him in the first place.

Ding. Ding.

Startled, she sloshed her coffee and glanced toward the front door. Who would be visiting her now?

She set down her mug. Maybe it was Dean?

She walked to the front door and looked out the window—Smiles Flower Delivery. She took a deep breath of relief—just sympathy flowers.

She opened the door and the sound of sleet hitting the pavement hummed through the air.

"Afternoon, ma'am, well, evening I guess." A freckle-faced high school boy holding a dozen roses smiled.

"Hello, sir."

"Sign here, please."

She took the clipboard and scribbled her name.

"Bad weather comin'." He handed her the flowers as she glanced at the sky. Yes, bad weather was definitely coming.

"Thank you. Be careful getting back."

"Yes, ma'am."

She watched him descend down the driveway before stepping back inside.

A smile spread across her face as she sniffed the red roses and walked to the kitchen. She set them on the table and plucked the card from the center.

A note to tell you I'm thinking of you. I'm so sorry for your loss. I love you.

Curtis.

Her breath caught. She turned the envelope over—the flowers were sent directly to her home address, not forwarded from the office like his last communication.

He knew where she lived. Which was virtually impossible because she was unlisted and had only been here a few months. There was no way her former client would know where she was, especially considering that her parents knew not to give her information out.

How the hell did he know?

A chill ran up her spine as she looked out the window.

Was he here?

Her hand trembled as she grabbed her cell phone from the counter, and without hesitation, she dialed Dean's number.

CHAPTER 19

DEAN HUNG UP the phone, grabbed his jacket and flicked off his office light. As he jogged down the station steps, he pulled his cell phone from his pocket.

"Jonas here."

"Jonas, were you able to confirm Curtis Eagan's whereabouts the night of Clint's murder?"

Pause. "Uh... hang on. I verified that he's not in jail and that he does, indeed, live in Belle Ridge. He lives in an apartment and works at a fast-food joint..."

"Where was he when Clint got shot?"

"I haven't gotten that far, yet. Kinda been doing the hundred other things you asked me to do."

"Figure it out, and for last night, too. I need to know today."

Jonas released a low sigh. "I'm on it."

"Thanks."

Click.

The sleet slid down his windshield as he pulled out of the parking lot and onto the main highway. Twilight crept onto the horizon, casting an eerie glow through the dark, ominous clouds. Traffic was crazy—everyone was out doing last minute grocery shopping and booze runs before the weather hit. He drove past the discount grocery store, which was packed to the street. Cars lined the square, with busy pedestrians going in and out of the post office, the hardware store and catching a last meal at Donny's Diner before being snowed in and forced to eat actual home cooked meals. Or meals from a can if the electricity went out, which he was very concerned would happen. In which case, the Berry Springs PD would be hammered with extra calls, on top of the calls they were bound to get regarding accidents.

It was almost seven in the evening by the time he pulled up the driveway to Heidi's house. The light posts that lined the driveway were lit and through the icy cloud of precipitation, the house looked majestic, sitting high on the mountaintop.

He parked behind Hayes's patrol car and walked to the front door. Before he could knock, the door opened.

She smiled.

His heart skipped a beat.

"Hi."

"Hi."

She stepped back and motioned him inside. "How's Trevor?"

Dean wiped his boots and slid out of his coat. "Pissed."

She raised her eyebrows. "Understandable."

"Where's Hayes?"

She grinned and nodded toward the sound of Eve's giggle in the kitchen.

Dean shook his head and his expression hardened. "Where's the flowers?"

"In the kitchen, come on."

He followed her down the hall, powerless against taking a quick glance at her perfectly-formed ass.

"Hey, Dean."

Eve turned and blushed. "Hi, detective."

He gave Hayes the side-eye before smiling at Eve. "Hi."

Heidi handed him the card, and the room fell silent as he read it. All eyes were on him. He turned to Hayes. "Can I talk to you for a second?"

Hayes nodded and followed Dean into the hall.

"You're released... which, for some odd reason, I don't think is what you wanted to hear."

"Since when?"

"Now. Go home, get some sleep. You've had, what, five or six hours in the last few days?"

"'Bout the same as you."

"Exactly. You need sleep. Go home and you can come back and flirt with Eve tomorrow."

Although he knew Hayes didn't want to leave his new crush, relief flashed in the rookie's eyes. The boy needed sleep, and he knew it.

"Alright. But what about Heidi?"

"I'll take care of it."

The phone rang in the kitchen.

"Sleep does sound good. Okay, I'll go say goodbye and call me tomorrow if you need anything."

"Will do."

They walked back into the kitchen as Eve hung up the phone. She turned to Heidi. "That was Jesse. We're going to run into town for a few things before the roads get too bad."

Heidi frowned. "I'm not sure that's such a great idea."

"We'll be quick."

"Okay, then. Be careful, and hurry. It'll get slick quick."

Hayes stepped next to Eve. "The roads are already bad, let me take you."

Dean shook his head. "No. Hayes, you need sleep. The last thing we need is you driving around on these roads tonight. Go home. It's not negotiable."

Eve put her hand on Hayes's back. "We'll be okay. I'll walk you out."

As Hayes and Eve left the room, Dean walked over to the roses and glowered down at them. "I'm confirming Eagan's whereabouts for the night of Clint's murder and last night as well."

She nodded and walked over to the table. "I don't know how he knows where I am, Dean."

Dean knew that if someone wanted to find someone else badly enough, there were plenty of ways to do it, and in his line of work, he'd seen it far too often.

Eve's voice called out from the front porch. *"Heidi, Jesse's outside, we'll be back."*

Heidi yelled back. "Okay, be careful!"

Pings against the window had Dean looking outside. The sleet was coming down in sheets.

Heidi followed his gaze and wrapped her arms around herself. They stared out the window, both sensing something. Something was in the air tonight.

She turned toward him. "You shouldn't stay long, I'm sure the ice is already sticking."

"I'll be alright." He had no plans of leaving her tonight.

She looked up at him, into his eyes. Her curly hair was down, with ringlets falling like a waterfall around her beautiful face.

"Would you like a drink?"

He nodded.

She walked to the liquor cabinet. "I've got all the usual suspects…"

"Whiskey, please." He needed something strong, to take the edge off.

"That actually sounds good." She pulled down two glasses. After adding a few ice-cubes, she poured the high dollar whiskey, handed him a glass and kept one for herself.

"Want to go to the den?"

"Sure."

He followed her down the hall, into the den. Tall windows looked out to the front yard where the sleet was falling like a blizzard. It was going to be a hell of a night.

She sat on the sofa. "Curtis is a troubled boy, no doubt about it, but I can't imagine him killing someone."

He walked over to the fireplace. "People do unexpected and indescribable things, Heidi." His eyes darkened as he gazed into the fire. "I've seen it."

His tone had her eyeing him, and in a voice as soft and comforting as a warm glass of milk, she asked, "What have you seen?"

He glanced at her, then quickly back at the fire. Nerves ran through his body. He didn't respond.

"Something happened to you."

He took a sip of whiskey, his mind racing to come up

with anything to change the subject, but for some damn reason, he couldn't think of a single thing.

"Tell me, Dean."

"This isn't about me, Heidi."

"Right now it is."

He looked into her eyes, so filled with compassion, and an eagerness to learn more about him. About *him*. It was her job to read people and help them, and right now, she was reading him like a book.

He cleared his throat and looked down. "I lost my dad, six years ago, well, seven as of yesterday. Yesterday was the anniversary."

"I'm so sorry."

He sipped again—a deep sip—praying the buzz would kick in and kill the emotions tumbling through his body.

When she sat silent, he continued, "He was shot in the head, between the eyes." His steely gaze cut to her. "Just like your husband, and Julie."

Her mouth fell open in shock.

"So yeah, I know all about people doing terrible things, unexpectedly."

She stood, walked over to him and grabbed his hand. Tears filled her eyes. "I'm so sorry, Dean."

"It's okay." No, it wasn't. It would never be okay until he killed the son of a bitch that killed his dad.

"Did they... you, find who did it?"

He clenched his jaw. "Not *yet*."

"Do you... do you think it could be the same person?"

"I don't know." He turned to her. "But I can promise you... I can promise you that I will find him, Heidi."

"You will, Dean. I know you will."

He blinked, surprised at her confidence in him. He hadn't realized it, but that was exactly what he needed to hear the last seven years. He needed to hear that he *would* find him. He needed encouragement, a true belief that one day this would be over, and he and his mother would get the closure that they so badly needed.

And this woman, that he'd only known for a few days, just gave that to him. Emotions flooded through his system; tears threatened to fill his eyes. He turned away, looked at the fire, and in every attempt to stay in control of himself, he changed the subject.

"So why don't you think Curtis did it?" He avoided eye contact, and the room stayed silent for a moment.

She finally cleared her throat—obviously understanding that he didn't want to talk about his father anymore—and said, "I don't know, but based on what I know of him, I just don't think it's him. Or Trevor, for that matter."

He exhaled the past away, clearing his head, and then said, "They both have motive… enough to look into."

She sipped her drink. "Curtis's parents abused him from birth until he was taken away. They were addicted to drugs, and his mother continued using while she was pregnant with him. He started getting into fights in elementary school—the writing was on the wall. He got a taste for violence and liked it. He liked the rush of it, but more than that he liked the feeling of power it gave him. For someone who had been powerless his whole life, kicking the shit out of someone else gave him the power. Or that's the way he saw it. It just takes someone one time to feel that adrenaline rush to become addicted."

"Sounds like an argument to support a theory that he did do it."

"No, I don't think he'd have the guts to murder someone—to take a life and face the consequences. Yes, Curtis beat people up, but the guilt and fear of the repercussions haunted him afterward. That was the majority of our conversations."

Dean sipped, in deep thought. He had two suspects—Trevor and Curtis—but his gut told him that he was missing something. Missing something that was right under his nose.

Heidi glanced at the fire and shivered. "The temperature's dropped. I'm going to turn up the heater and add some more wood to the fire."

"Why do you keep a fire going if you have central air and heat?"

"Do you have any idea how much it costs to heat and cool this place? It's nuts."

He smiled. She was frugal; and he was officially in love.

"I'll get the fire, you click up the heat."

"Sounds good."

He kneeled down and began working on the dwindling fire as she turned up the heat.

A minute later, she crouched down in front of the fireplace next to him. "It's really coming down outside."

He nodded, and after a second, asked, "Are we alone?"

She paused. "Yes."

A moment of silence slid by as they both stared into the fire, no doubt thinking the same thing.

He cleared his throat and forced the inappropriate

thoughts out of his head. "You'll need more wood. I'll get it." He stood.

"I'll help." She pushed off the floor.

He cocked his head and smirked. "It's pretty damn cold out there, Heidi."

"I'm pretty damn sure I can handle it, detective."

"Alright, then."

He plucked her coat from the rack and slid it on her, before putting on his own.

She grabbed her hat and opened the door.

"Be careful on the steps."

She rolled her eyes. "Yes, sir." She gripped his arm as they carefully stepped off the porch. "Jesse added a new woodpile today, this way."

They set out across the lawn, the frigid sleet raining down on them.

He scanned the area, keeping his head on a swivel as he walked up to the woodpile and began stacking logs in his arms, and Heidi's.

"I hope Eve and Jesse get back soon."

"They'd better. It's already slick." He looked at her and couldn't help but smile. She stood beside him, all bundled up, arms out and stacked with six logs. "Can you handle more?"

"Please." She rolled her eyes, again. "Stack me up."

"Alright." He grabbed two more of the smallest logs and carefully laid them in her arms—the stack now covering half her face. "Okay, that's enough big shot. You're going to topple over if I give you another."

She craned her neck to see from behind the wood. "I can take more."

He laughed. She was so *damn cute*. "Come on, Hercules, let's get back inside."

She took a step and her foot slipped out from under her. The wood few into the air and as Dean lunged forward to catch her, his foot slid, sending them both tumbling to the ground.

Laughter rang out from underneath him.

"Are you okay?"

She nodded, laughing so hard she couldn't speak.

He smiled and looked down at her, the ice melting down her beautiful face. She opened her eyes, met his gaze and for a moment they just stared at each other, smiling.

Like a moth to a flame, he leaned down and kissed her.

Butterflies burst in his stomach, a surge of electricity shot through his veins as his lips slid over hers. Her kiss was just as intense and passionate as he'd dreamed about in his sleep, and daydreamed about every second he was awake.

She pulled back, her breath short, her eyes wide with surprise.

His heart kicked as he looked down at her.

Like a dagger through the heart.

That moment, he realized that the only thing in the world he cared about was her. Amidst all the chaos, violence and sleepless nights, she was a force that replaced everything else. A force that melted him, took him completely over.

A force that he had to have, right that second.

He pushed off the ground, and as she started to sit up, he bent over and swept her off the ground, into his arms. She wrapped her arms around his neck and nuzzled into his chest as he carried her through the yard and into the house, leaving the wood behind. He felt the warmth of her lips on his neck, sending tingles up his spine.

"By the fire," she softly whispered in his ear.

The sleet pounded the windows outside as he laid her on the lush carpet in front of the crackling fire.

She looked up at him, the flames reflecting the yearning in her blue eyes. Lust, love, apprehension, nerves—he saw it all on her face.

"Heidi..." his voice was low and soft. "Are you sure?"

Her eyes twinkled. "Yes."

His heart dropped to the floor. It was going to happen. *It was happening.*

He stood, his massive body towering over her small frame. He kicked off his boots and pulled his shirt over his head. The warmth of the fire washed over his skin as he looked down at her, still hesitant. Was she ready? Emotionally ready?

As if reading his thoughts, she said, "Come here, Dean."

His heart started to pound as he bent down, and before he could even form a single thought, she reached up, pulled him down on top of her and began kissing him, wildly—a passionate kiss reflecting the release of the secret she'd clung to since she first laid eyes on him. The secret of her insatiable desire for him.

His clothes came off; hers were ripped off, their hands greedily caressing each other's bodies that they'd both spent hours fantasizing about.

His heart raced in his chest, his erection pulsating with frenzied desire—he was completely overcome by her. She was stunning, sexy, and her naked body was everything he'd imagined, and more.

His kissed her neck, savoring the sweet taste of her skin, and grabbed her plump breasts. She gripped his back and wrapped her bare legs around him. He felt the heat between her legs and lost all control. He became frantic, wanting to touch, lick, and taste every inch of her body.

He slid his tongue down her neck, to her chest, and as he took her nipple into his mouth, his hand swept down her side, down her stomach and onto her inner thigh.

She let out a low groan as his fingertips tickled her skin, lightly running along the soft hair of her inner lips. She squirmed beneath him, begging for more. He lingered a moment before sliding his fingers over her opening and onto her clit. Her body jolted at the mere touch, a rush of blood surged between his legs at her reaction.

He lightly circled the swollen bud, just barely touching the sensitive spot, and then inserted a finger into her wetness, rubbing her tight insides, in and out, in and out.

She tipped her head back and groaned.

"Oh, *Dean*."

He watched her close her eyes, her face squeeze with an impending orgasm. She was the sexiest thing he'd ever seen, and seeing her at the peak of satisfaction made him crazy.

He clenched his jaw, he was throbbing now. Rock-hard, between her legs.

He glided his finger out, and slid the wetness over her clit, again. Her breath picked up; she dug her fingernails into his back and he knew she was close.

Not yet.

He rubbed harder and faster and as she arched her back to orgasm, he pulled away and looked into her eyes.

"Are you ready?"

Her face was flushed, her lips full and supple, the fire in her eyes undeniable.

"*Yes.*"

He leaned down, kissed her lips, found her opening and slid into her. Shivers ran across his skin as she closed tightly around him, so warm. So wet.

He lingered for a moment, pressing deep inside her, embracing the feeling he'd waited what seemed his whole life for.

She arched her back impatiently, the passion shining through her eyes as she looked at him.

He slowly slid out, kissed her, and slid back in, savoring each smooth stroke.

She met his rhythm and their bodies molded together, into one.

Sweat beaded on his back as he slid in and out, faster and faster.

Her nails pressed into his shoulders.

"*Oh, Dean.*" The breathy whisper against his ear sent him into a whirlwind.

He plunged deeper, feeling more and more wetness with each thrust. The throbbing turned into a hot tingling as the sensation began to build. He pushed harder, deeper inside of her, his heart feeling like it was about to burst out of his chest.

Her breath picked up and she started to tense and squeeze around his cock.

"I'm close, *don't stop.*"

His head started to spin, the world became a blur.

"Oh, *Dean.*"

She arched her back. *"Dean."* Her body pulsated around him, a warm rush of liquid sliding over him. Stars burst in his eyes, his body tightened and he released everything he had into her.

She lay limp beneath him, gazing up at him with tired, exhausted and satisfied eyes.

He blinked—completely disoriented from the earth-shattering orgasm he'd just had. He blew out a breath, leaned down and kissed her sweaty forehead. She smiled, he smiled, and rolled off.

Suddenly, a scratching noise sounded from outside.

His head shot up, glancing at the front door.

Heidi grabbed her shirt.

"You said we're alone?"

She nodded, her face pulled tight with concern. "Yes, Jesse and Eve are in town and you've got Trevor at the station."

He grabbed his boxers, slid into them. "Stay here, I'll be right back." He plucked his Glock off the floor and slowly walked to the doorway, and listened.

Again, *scratch.*

He looked back at Heidi, who was pulling on her clothes, then quickly stepped into the hall. He glanced out the window where sheets of ice did nothing to help the visibility.

Suddenly, from outside the front door, a low whimper. *Gus.*

He rolled his eyes, lowered his gun and opened the

door. Gus barreled inside, whimpering, slinging ice and snow all over the floor.

He kneeled down. "You okay, buddy?"

The freezing dog whimpered and licked his hand.

"You're alright. It's too cold out there isn't it?"

He heard Heidi chuckle as he glanced out the open door. Ice covered every inch of the ground, compounding as the minutes dragged on. The sky was as black as ink.

A chill ran up his spine.

He narrowed his eyes and looked out to the dark woods and something turned in his gut; a warning signal.

An instinct that something terrible was about to happen.

CHAPTER 20

FEELING LIKE SHE was floating on air, Heidi poured another drink of whiskey, curled up on the chaise lounge next to the fire and watched the sleet coming down. Gus curled at her ankles, just a few feet away from where she had just had the best, mind-blowing sex she had ever had in her life.

Gazing out the window, she softly ran her finger down her neck, where Dean's lips had been just an hour earlier. His lush, soft lips that tasted like whiskey. She smelled him on her skin, that indescribable scent of a man.

Her mind was mush and her body still weak from the orgasm that had rocketed through her.

She sipped her drink and glanced at the loaded pistol on the coffee table that Dean had left her before he'd gone outside to do a perimeter check, an hour ago.

Ring, ring.

She reached forward and plucked her cell phone off the table.

"Hello?"

"Heidi, it's Eve."

"Hey, are you guys back?"

"No, they freakin' closed the mountain."

"You're kidding."

"Nope, we were two cars back and they closed it. Unpassable from the ice, apparently."

"Oh, no. Are you still with Jesse?"

"Yeah, he has a key to Trevor's place in town so we're here for now. He just ran out to get some fast-food."

"Okay, I'm so sorry, but I'm glad you're safe."

"Me, too. Anyway, I just wanted to call and let you know, so you wouldn't worry."

"Thank you. Keep me updated, okay?"

"Okay. Are you okay?"

She glanced at the gun. "Yes, everything's good here."

"Good. Talk soon."

"Bye."

Click.

Just then, Dean walked through the front door with his cell phone pressed to his ear. As he kicked the ice off his boots, Gus jumped up to greet him and Heidi strained to listen to the call.

"How many kids... *dammit*... okay... I'll call you back." He slid his phone into his pocket and sighed as he walked into the den.

The look on his face had her sitting up in her chair. "Is everything okay?"

"They closed the mountain, but before they did, they let a single woman with three kids through, and of course, she's off the road now, stuck in a ditch."

Heidi stood. "Oh, no, are they okay?"

"Physically yes, but the mom is scared as shit and bottom line, those kids will freeze to death if they don't get home."

"You've got to go get them."

He frowned as he looked down at her.

She put her hand on her hip and cocked an eyebrow. "Dean, give me a break, I'll be fine. You've got to go take care of those kids."

He glanced outside. "They're just a few miles down the road. She said she lives close to where they're stuck."

"So then it's close. Go... and be careful, okay?"

He paused. "You're coming with me."

She laughed. "Okay, you, me, a woman and three kids are going to fit nicely in your truck." She ruffled Gus's ears. "I've got Gus and a gun, I'm all set. And besides, you said the mountain is closed, right? It's impossible for anyone to get out here."

He hesitated, concern written all over his face.

She opened the door. "Go. The sooner you go, the sooner you get back."

He leaned forward, kissed her forehead and lightly grabbed her face. "Keep that gun with you, okay? And your cell phone, close, at all times."

She nodded, and lightly kissed his lips.

He smiled, winked. "I'll be right back, okay?"

"Okay, see you soon."

She locked the door behind him and watched him walk to his truck, muttering profanities as he slid on a patch of ice. She laughed and waved as his taillights faded into the blackness.

It astounded her that she could find a laugh, or even a little humor during such a dark time in her life. But love has a way of finding the light in even the darkest of places. He was a distraction, too, a six-foot-four muscular, hunky distraction.

She double-checked the locks and looked down at Gus, whose tail was wagging wildly.

"Well, it's just you and me for a little while, buddy."

He whimpered.

"Okay, I see you want a cookie." She patted her thigh and turned toward the kitchen. "Come on, stinker."

Gus darted down the hall.

The house was quiet, eerily so. She was used to Clint, or Eve, Jesse or Trevor making noise somewhere. Or, at least, the white noise of the television in the background, which she'd intentionally left off after seeing the headline, *The Novak Family Tragedy*, at the top of the morning news.

She stepped into the kitchen, gave Gus a cookie and instead of refilling her whiskey, she opted for a small glass of red wine.

She sipped, inhaled, and leaned against the counter.

Gus devoured the cookie, then sauntered to the back door, and let out a whimper.

"You just went outside."

He whimpered again.

She shook her head. "Alright, then."

She let him out and watched him dart into the woods.

The moment she shut the door—darkness.

"Oh *no*." The electricity had gone out. She froze, blinking a few times to allow her eyes to adjust.

Dammit. Her cell phone and gun were in the den.

Damn, damn, damn.

She felt around the pitch-black kitchen for candles, but

then remembered that Clint didn't like candles; he said they kicked up his allergies.

She'd brought a box of them with her when she'd moved in, but they had been tucked in the basement, far away from Clint's sensitive nose.

She turned, paused. The basement was the one part of the house that was unfinished and in shambles, and there was no way in hell she was going down there with only her cell phone as a light.

She reached for the wall and slowly began walking down the hall. She was halfway to the den when the lights turned on.

She blew out an exhale. "Thank God."

She was standing directly in front of the basement door and after a quick hesitation, she pushed it open—she'd need the candles if the electricity went out again.

The musty smell of a cellar floated up the long, narrow wooden staircase.

She flicked on the light, which only illuminated about half the space, gripped the railing and with each step, the staircase creaked and groaned beneath her.

It was creepy, and *freezing*.

Just get the candles, and get the hell out.

She stepped off the staircase and looked around, trying to remember where she'd put her boxes. Electrical wiring ran across the walls, which were covered in insulation. Thick, wooden posts supported the floor above. And boxes—hundreds of boxes and storage containers were stacked to the ceiling. It was a mess, and quite frankly, it made her skin crawl.

She let out a squeak as a rat scurried across the concrete floor.

"*Dammit.* Okay, screw this. Way too creepy for me."

As she turned to walk up the steps, she spotted her boxes in the far corner, shaded by darkness. She let go of the railing and quickly walked across the room, maneuvering between the stacks.

"Okay, now which one was it," she whispered as she began unstacking each box.

The smell of fresh, moldy earth filled her nose and she straightened, and looked around. Her eyes landed on a pile of dirt and small, broken slabs of concrete in the corner.

What the hell?

She set down the box, squeezed in-between two stacks of storage bins and carefully stepped to the corner. Her eyes widened as she looked down—just inches from a shovel was a hole in the earth, about three feet deep, and buried in the dirt was an old, silver safe.

"What the *hell?*"

She kneeled down and leaned forward for a better look.

WHACK!

Pain shot through her skull before blackness engulfed her.

***

Dean gripped the steering wheel as he slowly navigated around a tight corner that hugged the edge of a jagged cliff. The solid three hours of sleet had finally started to slow, but was replaced by blankets of falling snow.

Warnings beeped from the local radio station reminding people to stay home, and off the roads.

His heartbeat was a steady pounding in his chest. Not just because of the weather conditions and the fact that he was driving on a road with a two-hundred foot drop-off, but because he hated leaving Heidi. Alone.

He'd been gone thirty minutes already and hadn't even made it a mile down the road. Visibility was shit.

He guessed this whole ordeal was going to cost him over three hours. And that was three hours longer than he cared to leave Heidi.

He clenched his jaw, the impatience gnawing at him.

His cell phone rang and nerves shot through his body as he glanced down. He exhaled a breath of relief when he saw that it wasn't Heidi calling to tell him something was wrong.

"Walker here."

"Dean, it's Wesley."

Something in Wesley's voice made his stomach sink. "What's up?"

"Last night a guy came in and traded in a few guns, for some cash and a new pistol. I didn't think too much of it until I started going through them, to clean them up."

"Okay…"

"One of his guns was a Colt 1911."

Dean's heart stopped.

"Out of curiosity, I just compared the markings on the casing you left with me yesterday—the one you found on Mrs. Novak's land—to the barrel of the gun, and I'll be a son of a bitch, it's a match. So then, I checked the bullet that Jessica pulled from Clint's head and it's a fucking match, too. Dean, I've got your murder weapon."

Dean hit the brakes. "What's the guy's name?"

"Jesse Reid."

CHAPTER 21

DEAN SLAMMED THE truck in reverse and pressed down on the accelerator, backing down the road with not much more than his rearview mirror and sense of direction guiding him through the curves.

His heart raced.

Jesse. *Fucking Jesse.*

He finally found a spot to turn around and slid on a patch of black ice before taking off toward Heidi's. He picked up the phone and dialed her number.

No answer.

He tried again.

"Come on, Heidi, pick up, *pick up.*"

No answer.

His skin tingled with nerves. Something was wrong, he knew it in his gut.

The snow blanketed his windshield, making it impossible to see more than a few yards ahead of him. His knuckles were as white as paper, his face flushed with emotion as he pressed the accelerator harder.

He called again.

No answer.

He slid around a corner, fish-tailed and landed in a ditch.

"*Dammit!*" He pounded the steering wheel, rage burning through his system.

He had to get to her, he had to get to her now.

He shoved the truck into reverse, slid back a few inches and then slowly accelerated. The truck edged up the ditch, then slid back down.

"Fuck!"

Calm down, Dean.

He released an exhale, attempting to calm his nerves, and tried again, with the same result.

"*Son of a bitch!*" He peered through the windshield, contemplating.

He tried one more time to get out of the ditch, with no luck. He only had one option now.

He slammed the truck into park, turned off the engine, grabbed his cell phone and Glock, and jumped out, into the freezing weather.

The snow stung his face, his ears, his hands and almost blinded him as he ran down the road. He estimated he was less than a mile from Heidi's, which would take him just under eight minutes in normal conditions.

But not a fucking blizzard.

The ice-cold air burned his lungs as he pressed on, running up the mountain.

The image of her face popped into his head. She was in trouble. He knew it.

He clenched his fists and pushed into a sprint, and finally her driveway came into view. Adrenaline gave him the extra momentum he needed as he flew up the driveway, and pulled the Glock from his belt.

Suddenly, something jumped out of the woods beside him.

Gus.

What the fuck was Gus doing outside? He'd given Heidi clear instructions to keep him inside.

The dog ran up on his heels, followed him onto the porch and whined as Dean turned the doorknob.

Locked.

"Fuck!" He looked in the window and yelled her name. "Heidi?"

No answer.

He banged on the door and yelled again.

No answer.

He turned, his eyes darting around the porch—stopping on a block of wood.

"Get back Gus."

Dean grabbed the wood, took a quick inhale and busted through the front window.

"Heidi?" He jumped inside, ran into the den and noticed her cell phone and gun on the table.

"Heidi?"

Silence.

He turned on his heel and ran down the hall, his eyes landing on the open basement door. Heart racing, he flew down the stairs, gun in hand. As he reached the bottom of the staircase, he saw movement to his right.

Jesse turned, shovel in hand, and froze in front of Heidi's crumpled body on the floor.

Wild fury shot through him as he jumped off the staircase and lunged toward Jesse, knocking the shovel out of his hand and slamming his fist into his face. Blood splattered on the wall. The punch was answered back by a knee ramming into Dean's gut, followed by a right hook.

The metallic taste of blood filled Dean's mouth, and his adrenaline spiked, his eyes cold as ice as he threw himself on Jesse. Boxes crashed to the ground. Fists flying, they stumbled backwards, until Jesse's back was up against the cold, concrete wall. Dean towered over him, more than double his size. He pinned Jesse against the wall and punched him repeatedly, blind with rage. His hands wrapped around Jesse's throat.

Jesse's arms went limp, his eyeballs bulged from his face.

Dean's heartbeat thudded in his ears as he watched Jesse's eyes begin to glaze over.

Let go, Dean. Let go.

He gripped harder.

Let go, Dean.

He released his grip and Jesse's body slid to the ground.

"Heidi!"

He jumped over to Heidi's motionless body and fell to his hands and knees. Her hair was matted with blood, her face pale, her eyes closed.

"Oh, my God."

He picked up her wrist and felt a faint pulse. She was alive.

He grabbed his cell phone.

"Dispatch, I need a medic to nine twenty-eight County Road 43. The Novak Estate. *Now.*"

"Sir, the mountain has been closed."

"Then send a helicopter. Call Dr. Buckley directly, tell him I need his help."

"Yes, sir."

Dean clicked off the phone and scooped Heidi into his arms as Jesse darted up the staircase.

* * *

Dean let out an exhale as the hum from the helicopter approaching cut through the silence. He leaned down, kissed Heidi's forehead and jogged outside.

The helicopter landed in the back field, yards from Heidi's back patio. Dean jogged through the snow as the propellers cut off.

"Ain't no way in hell we're going back tonight." Dr. Buckley jumped out, bag in hand.

"Buckley, I can't thank you enough. She's inside."

Just then, Hayes, Eve and Trevor jumped out of the back.

Dean turned. "What the..."

Hayes stepped forward, his eyes sharp and intense. "Eve called me; I picked her up and we were at the station when the call came through. Under the circumstances, I let Trevor go. Oh, and Willard got the mom and kids that were stranded on the mountain home safe. How's Heidi?"

Dean turned and led the way through the snow, as Gus darted across the patio and fell into step beside him.

"She's not good, unconscious. But she's got a pulse, and it's picked up since I got her."

"Jesse?"

"He took off."

"Did you see him?"

"Just his body fly up the staircase. I didn't want to leave Heidi's side."

Trevor glanced over his shoulder. "I'll go check his cabin."

"Take Hayes with you."

Hayes turned to Eve as he grabbed the gun from his coat. "You stay inside, okay? Stay with Dean and Dr. Buckley. I'll be back."

Fear clouded her face, and he grabbed her hand. "I'll be back."

"Hayes, let's go."

Hayes turned and jogged behind Trevor to the ATV shed.

Dr. Buckley looked at Dean. "One of the staff did it?"

He nodded.

The doctor shook his head, "I'm sorry, but there was always something… weird with this family."

"Did you know Jesse?"

"A little, just from casual meetings. Seemed normal."

"No signs at all? Nothing that would make you think he would do something like this?"

"No, not one. You got any ideas?"

"I've still got to figure that out, but right now, Heidi's our number one priority."

Dean pushed through the back door and led Dr. Buckley into the den. He stood back and watched the doctor get to work. He had tunnel vision—nothing else in the world mattered to him, other than ensuring that Heidi was going to be okay.

The minutes dragged on as he stood stoically next to the fire, his eyes locked on her beautiful face.

Finally, Dr. Buckley pushed off the floor and turned to Dean.

"She's got a concussion, and the gash on her head is going to need stitches, but she's going to be okay."

Dean took a deep breath, surprised at the emotions flowing through him. "Can you stitch her up here? Now?"

"Of course, I'll need to shave a small area on her head and I can easily stitch it up; it's not deep. The blow was the worst of it."

He grit his teeth. He should have strangled the son of a bitch.

"The number one thing she needs right now is rest. For at least a few days. I'll keep a close eye on her and if she needs to go to the hospital tomorrow morning, we'll get her there. But there's no way in hell I can take the helo out in this blizzard."

"Understood, and thank you. Seriously," he shook his hand, "I can't thank you enough."

Dr. Buckley looked around. "There's certainly worse places to be stuck. Damn, this is a nice place."

Dean's cell phone rang.

"Yeah?"

"Dean, it's Hayes. Jesse isn't at his cabin and there's no sign of him."

"Keep looking."

"Yes, sir."

Dean slid his phone into his pocket and gazed out the window.

"What?"

"No sign of Jesse."

Dr. Buckley followed his gaze. "Lots of snow out there. Pretty much impossible not to leave tracks."

"You read my mind."

"Go."

Dean looked at him.

"*Go.* She's going to be okay. I won't leave her side. Go."

Dean took a deep breath and grabbed his gun. "I'll be back."

"Go."

CHAPTER 22

DEAN NARROWED HIS steely eyes, clenched his jaw and tightened the grip on his Glock. He looked around, into the dark night.

Wind whipped around him, the snow falling in blankets on the ground. The air was ice-cold but he didn't feel it. In fact, adrenaline had his cheeks flushing.

He stepped off the porch and scanned the ground.

A faded boot track sank into the snow just ahead of him, surrounded by droplets of blood. And, sure enough, another track, followed by another. And, more blood.

Like an animal on the hunt, he took off into the night, his flashlight leading the way.

The snow blinded him, stinging his eyes and sliding down his back.

With laser focus, he jogged across the yard, following each footprint until they disappeared into the woods.

Shit.

He took a deep breath, stepped into the pitch-black woods, and immediately found another track, alongside broken twigs. Luck was on his side.

He took off in a jog. The adrenaline to find the man that almost killed the woman he'd fallen in love with pumped through his veins.

He pushed on, deeper and deeper into the woods, following tracks and blood drippings. Finally, he came to a fence, with fields beyond.

Old man Williams's land.

Just then, through the snow, he saw the flicker of a flashlight in the distance. He jumped over the fence and took off in a sprint. As he got closer, he drew his gun.

"Stop right there!"

He raised his gun as the figure stopped, turned, and pointed a sawed-off shotgun right in his face.

"Mr. Williams, drop your gun."

Old man Williams squinted and leaned forward. "I'll be damned. Dean Walker, that you?"

"Yes, sir, drop that God damned gun before I shoot it out of your hands."

Williams dropped his arms. "Oh. Sorry, son."

Dean dropped his gun and looked the old man over. His thick beard, and thicker eyebrows, were covered in snow. A brown plaid hunting cap topped his balding head, and a thick jacket covered his jean overalls, which were tucked into a pair of snow boots.

"What the hell are you doing out here?"

"I's fixin' to ask you the same question."

"You first."

"I saw someone. Damned trespassers again."

"You saw someone, just now?"

"Yep."

Dean's heart skipped a beat. "Where?"

"I saw the flicker of a light in the barn." He motioned across the field. "Over there."

Dean looked at the old, dilapidated barn about fifty yards ahead, barely visible in the snow.

"When exactly?"

"'Bout as long ago as it took me to pull my boots on, get into my jacket and grab my gun."

Considering old man Williams age, and how far he'd walked from his house, that was probably twenty minutes ago.

It had to be Jesse.

"Mr. Williams, I want you to get back to your house, right now."

The old man narrowed his eyes. "Who's out there? This here's my land and I got every right to protect it."

"You're damn right you do, sir, but I'm here now, and this is my fight. I want you to get back to the house, lock the door and keep your gun handy."

The look in Dean's eyes had Williams taking a step back. "Alright, son. You let me know what happens, alright?"

"Yes, sir. Go on, now."

As Williams turned and began walking to his house, Dean ran across the field, his gut telling him that every step was bringing him closer to Jesse.

As he neared the barn, he slowed his pace and hunkered down. He paused at the door—which was opened just a crack—and listened.

Silence.

As far as he could tell, the barn was pitch-black inside.

He clicked on his flashlight, raised it alongside his

gun, slid his finger onto the trigger and stepped inside. The smell of manure singed his nose.

Suddenly, a flash from the side.

Dean spun on his heel just as Jesse leapt through the air.

They tumbled to the ground and as Jesse scrambled to get away—*like a little bitch*—Dean grabbed his shoulders, ripping his shirt in the process, and pulled him down, and flipped him on his stomach.

The flashlight tumbled to the ground, illuminating a deep scar on Jesse's shoulder.

An old bullet wound.

He shoved the barrel of his gun into Jesse's neck. "You fucking move, I'll shoot you right here, you fucking son of a bitch."

In one swift movement, he cuffed Jesse's dirty hands behind his back, pulled him to a stance and pointed the gun to his head.

"Back to the house. Let's go."

* * *

"Dean?" Hayes lingered in the hallway, covered head to toe in snow and mud.

Dean turned to Dr. Buckley. "I'll be right back."

He met Hayes in the hall.

"She okay?"

"Concussion and stitches, but she'll be okay. You get Jesse tied up?"

"Yeah... I, uh, had to sedate him a bit."

"With your fist?"

"Well, Trevor's, but yeah. We put him down in the basement… and I think you're going to want to see this."

Dean frowned. What had he missed?

"Can you come now?"

Dean glanced over his shoulder at Heidi, who was sleeping soundly, with Dr. Buckley and Gus at her side.

He nodded and followed Hayes down into the basement where Eve paced next to a stack of boxes and Trevor was crouched down over something in the corner.

"Did you see what Jesse was doing when you came down?"

"No. I kicked his ass and got Heidi."

Dean followed Hayes to the corner of the room, where a silver safe lay next to a deep hole in the ground.

Hayes motioned to the safe. "We're assuming it was buried in this hole, based on the dirt and shit all over it. It was unlocked…"

Trevor opened the lid, where bundles of hundred dollar bills lay neatly stacked inside.

Dean raised his eyebrows.

"Yeah, a shit-ton of money. We're thinking close to a million bucks, cash."

Dean frowned and crouched down. "Whose money, I wonder? Jesse's?"

Trevor shook his head. "I don't think so. I think it was Earl's."

He glanced over his shoulder. "Why do you think that?"

"There's been rumors that Earl hid money all over the property—he never trusted banks. At least that's what I heard."

"Okay, so where does Jesse come in?"

Trevor shrugged. "Not sure, but I just told Hayes, I remember a few days before Clint was killed, Jesse and I were feeding the cows and he randomly asked me what I would do if I came across a lot of money. It was a casual conversation, I didn't think anything of it. We talked about it for a while, daydreaming what we would do and such. He said he'd take off to Mexico and buy a place on the ocean. Looking back, he was acting funny—edgy, hyper-like."

Suddenly, behind them, Eve gasped.

Dean turned, cocked an eyebrow.

Her mouth dropped open. "Oh, my, *God.*"

Hayes grabbed her arm. "What?"

The blood drained from her face. "The other day, um, last week I guess… I was cleaning and I went into Clint's office, and Jesse was there, which was actually kind of odd that he would be in there in the first place." She paused, as if recounting the moment in her head. "He was behind Clint's desk, and when he saw me, he looked all surprised. We made small talk and then he left. I didn't think anything of it and I just kept doing my chores. Well, eventually, I made my way over to the desk and," she looked down, "I shouldn't have looked, but the Novak's bank statements were sitting out, so I looked."

"It's okay, keep going."

"And lying right next to the papers was Earl's will."

The room fell silent for a moment.

Hayes looked at Dean. "How much you wanna bet that this hidden stash, along with its location was included in that will."

Dean glanced down at the open safe. "I'd bet every damn penny in here. Eve, go get that will."

Under a minute later, Eve jumped off the staircase, with the will in her hand, and sure enough, the amount and location of the money was included in it.

Hayes shook his head. "But why kill for it? Why not just steal it and hit the road?"

Dean looked back down at the will. "Look here," he pointed to the paper. "It says that the code to the safe had been passed to the inheritors. So Earl gave his kids the code before he died." He leaned up. "Security code. Jesse needed the damn security code."

"And I'll bet when Clint wouldn't give it to him, he shot him."

"And then went after Julie, who is the only other person who would know the code."

"But why Heidi?"

Dean's eyes narrowed, his fists clenched. "Tying up loose ends."

CHAPTER 23

DEAN'S HEART RACED as he bent over and peered down at the table, illuminated with fluorescent lights. "Dude, you've got to quit breathing down my neck."

"Sorry." He straightened, wiped the sheen of sweat from his brow and began pacing the room. Well, *room* was a bit of an exaggeration. Dean was in Wesley's basement, which had been turned into a makeshift gun manufacturing shop. Wesley had another, more professional facility on his land but he preferred to do most of his work in his basement, under his house. Especially with almost two feet of snow outside.

Dean took a few silent deep breaths to calm his nerves while he waited impatiently.

With a magnifying glass to his eye, Wesley was hunched over a bullet casing, and Jesse's Colt 1911. "And you're a hundred percent sure that this casing was found where your dad was shot, seven years ago?"

"A hundred and ten percent. Found it myself."

"Okay." Wesley pulled the light closer.

As he paced, Dean's gaze landed on the old TV in the background.

"... main roads are still closed and it is strongly advised to stay home and avoid getting out. County maintenance crews are working around the clock to plow the roads... And now, to our top story... The body of a Vermont woman was found murdered last night on Summit Mountain. A relative of the victim, unidentified at this time, was also found at the scene, beaten unconscious. She is currently recovering, and is expected to survive. The police have arrested a person of interest, although his identity has yet to be released. As always, we will keep you updated on this developing story."

Dean's stomach clenched. It had been less than twelve hours since he'd almost lost Heidi and he was running on no sleep and pure adrenaline.

Somewhere in the middle of the night, the snow let up, and Heidi had finally awakened, to Dean right by her side. It was a moment he'd never forget. She opened her eyes, blinked the blurriness away, looked directly at him and smiled the sweetest, most beautiful smile. Relief flooded him. She was going to be okay.

After waking the doctor to check on her, and then feeding her a bowl of soup, Dean rubbed her head until she fell back to sleep.

At morning's first light, Dr. Buckley, Hayes, and Jesse—who had remained cuffed and tied in the basement all night—fired up the helicopter and flew back to town. Dean instructed Hayes to lock Jesse in a cell, while Buckley went back to the hospital to make his rounds.

After ensuring Heidi was feeling better, and Eve would

stay by her side, Dean went—correction, *slid*—into town to take care of business.

Fuck the snow. Fuck the ice. He wanted to ensure that Jesse never saw the light of day again... and he had something else he needed to check on, too.

Wesley straightened, took off his magnifying glasses and pushed the light away from the table.

Dean crossed the room in two swift steps.

"Well?"

Wesley, turned and met Dean's gaze. His eyes narrowed, his jaw set. He waited a moment, as if choosing his words carefully, then said, "It matches."

Dean's heart stopped.

"The markings match. The bullet that killed your dad was shot from this gun."

His chest seized, his breath stopped.

"Dean, Jesse killed your dad."

Rage pumped like fuel through his veins, feeding the violent and heinous thoughts that ran through his head. He sped carelessly down the icy roads; his eyes wild, his jaw clenched, his grip so tight around the steering wheel that he was surprised it didn't pop off.

Memories of the night that Jesse Reid killed his father flooded his head. Memories of his mother, weeping in his arms. Memories of the police interviews, the funeral, the hole that was left in his family's legacy. A hole that would never be filled again.

It had been seven years. Seven years without closure.

Seven years of sleepless nights, replaying every second of that night, trying to put the pieces of the puzzle together. Seven years of looking at every man who walked through the station doors, wondering if he was the one who murdered his father. Seven years of checking every single confiscated gun to see if it was a match. Seven years of his mother living the life of a lonely widow.

Seven years of him plotting how he would kill the man who killed his dad.

He'd imagined putting a bullet between the man's eyes, just like was done to his dad. But no, that would be too quick. He imagined slicing his throat, but no, that would be too quick too. He imagined beating the man to death with a butt of a gun, but no, he needed more than that.

He imagined tying him up, his wrists and ankles, sitting him in front of a mirror and sawing his fingers off one by one, so the man could never hold another gun for the rest of his life. And then, he would drag him out to the field—to the same bonfire where he and his father took their last sip of whiskey together before he was brutally shot—tie the man to a tree, douse him in gasoline and set him on fire and watch him burn to death.

And then, just for good measure, he'd send a bullet through the charred skull.

A poetic ending for the devil that destroyed his family.

His mouth was practically salivating with anticipation of looking into Jesse's eyes when his phone rang.

As he slid around a corner, he yanked it from the console.

Through his teeth, he muttered, "Walker here."

"Hey... it's Jonas."

"Yeah?"

"Uh… I just… you okay, man?"

"Yeah, what do you want?"

"I got the surveillance footage from Tad's. Sure enough, it's Jesse, buying the same fertilizer that was found on the tire tracks next to Clint's body, and the foot tracks on Heidi's porch."

Perfect. But it wasn't enough. He wanted Jesse to pay for murdering his father as well, and he wouldn't rest until that happened.

Jonas continued, "Also, I got the phone dump from Jesse's cell. He sent a text to Clint the evening Clint was murdered."

"What did it say?"

"Asked him to go for a drive, that he needed to talk to him."

Dean inhaled, trying to focus. "This is good. Nice work, Jonas."

"Thanks. You still with Heidi?"

"No, I'm on the way to the station… got something I need to do."

"What? How the hell did you make it off the mountain? It was still closed last I heard."

"See you soon."

"Dean?"

"Yeah?"

"Be careful."

Click.

His heart felt like it was about to explode as he scaled the station steps, two-by-two. His nails dug into his skin from his clenched fists. He pushed through the front doors with tunnel vision.

"Whoa…" Wide-eyed, Ellen from dispatch jumped out of his way as he strode past her. He didn't even see her.

The noise from the bullpen was nothing but a buzz in his ears.

He keyed in his code and pushed through the door leading to the three prison cells inside the department.

"Hey, Dean, to what do I owe…"

Dean grabbed the keys from the wall. He didn't hear the guard, he didn't see the guard.

"Dean, you okay?"

His skin tingled with adrenaline as he walked up to Jesse's cage. As soon as he laid eyes on him, Jesse stood, wide-eyed, as if he knew what was coming.

The guard crossed the room. "Hey, uh, Dean…"

His hands were steady as he unlocked the cell.

He opened the door and for a split second, paused and stared into the eyes of the man that shot his father.

Seven years of rage overcame him as he leapt into the cage and slammed his fist into Jesse's face.

"Dean! *Get me back-up in the cells! Now!*"

The sound of Jesse's nose breaking echoed through the air, blood splattered the gray cell walls, teeth bounced off the floor.

"*Dean!*"

It took three men to pull Dean off the man who killed his father, and tried to kill the woman he'd fallen madly in love with.

CHAPTER 24

HEIDI OPENED HER eyes, blinked a few times and glanced out the window. The bright afternoon sun reflected off the snow-covered mountains. Icicles, four-inches each in length, clung to the windowsill.

It looked like a winter wonderland.

"Good morning."

Butterflies awoke in her stomach at the sound of his voice. She turned her head to see Dean, sitting on the edge of her bed.

She smiled.

"Good morning."

He edged closer to her. "How are you feeling?"

"Better... much better. And hungry."

He smiled, so big. "Ah, that makes me so happy. Eve's ready to cook you whatever you want."

"What time is it?"

"Almost three in the afternoon."

She pushed herself up on her elbows. "Oh, my gosh, I can't believe it."

He put his hand over hers. "It's good. You're doing exactly what you need to do."

She glanced out the window. "It's been two days, right?"

"A little over forty-eight hours since it happened."

She shook her head. "I'm so sorry, I'm so sorry I've slept almost the whole time."

He slid even closer to her, and kissed her forehead. "Don't apologize, your body's healing. Your head is healing." Pause. "I'd like to take you in to see Dr. Buckley in a few hours, just to check on the stitches and for a quick x-ray."

She looked at him, panic suddenly washing over her face. "What's happened? Where's Jesse? What's happened?"

He swallowed the lump in his throat and forced a smile. A part of him had hoped she'd forgotten about what happened—hoping the blow to the head would erase the terrible events from that night.

"Everything's going to be okay... let's get some food in you first, before we talk about everything."

She grabbed his hand. "But what about Julie's funeral? I've got emails to answer and calls to make—"

"Heidi, stop. Eve has been in constant contact with Julie's husband—they've worked together and everything is finalized for both Clint and Julie's funeral. It's all taken care of and will be okay."

She inhaled deeply and nodded.

"Let's get you some coffee, then breakfast."

"Okay."

After wrapping her in her favorite terry cloth robe, he insisted on carrying her down the staircase. As they stepped onto the first floor, the warm smell of wood burning and the faint crackle of the fireplace echoed through the room.

"*Heidi!*" Eve darted down the hall, wiping her hands on her apron.

She smiled. Something about that bubbly blonde made her heart swell.

"How are you? I have so much food for you! Coffee first?"

"Yes, please."

Eve grabbed her hand, guided her down the hall as Dean followed closely behind.

"Here, sit. Or, would you like to sit next to the fire in the den?"

She looked at Dean, who was smiling—obviously loving how Eve was falling all over herself to take care of her.

"Actually, yeah, I'd love to curl up next to the fire."

"Okay, you go in there, and I'll bring you coffee and then you'll tell me what you want to eat."

"Thank you so much, Eve."

"It's absolutely my pleasure." She frowned, tears filling her eyes. "You've been through so much."

Dean grabbed her hand. "Come on, I've got the fire going for you."

He led her into the den, eased her into her favorite chair and covered her with a blanket.

Eve scurried into the room. "Here you go, Heidi. Do you know what you'd like to eat?"

Heidi sipped her coffee—it was heaven. She looked at Eve and smiled. "So good, thank you. Let me get this cup in me and then we'll figure out food."

"Okay, just yell at me." Eve looked at Dean. "I'll leave you two alone."

As Eve left the room, Heidi took another sip and turned to Dean.

"Tell me. Tell me everything."

Dean lightly inhaled, the stress of the last forty-eight hours was written all over his face. He looked worn, tired and stressed. Although she'd slept most of the last two days, Eve had been giving her updates when Dean wasn't by her side, and she knew that he'd been burning the candle at both ends, trying to take care of everything.

His eyes narrowed as he gazed into the fire, taking a moment to compose his thoughts. She waited patiently.

Finally, he looked at her. "Jesse is locked up and won't see the light of day for a very long time. After we piled a mound of evidence in front of him, he confessed to killing Clint, Julie and coming after you, for the money he found in the basement."

"What money?"

Dean explained how Jesse had stumbled upon Earl's will, learning of the hidden money. "So the night that he killed Clint, he'd told him that he needed to talk to him—go for a drive—and that's when he demanded that Clint give him the code to the hidden safe, and when Clint refused, he shot him, kicked him out of the truck and Clint rolled off the cliff."

Her eyes rounded. "How much money was worth killing for?"

"Just over five-hundred-thousand dollars."

Heidi's heart clenched hearing the story. Her hands began to tremble. How many breakfasts and dinners had she shared with Jesse? How many casual conversations? How many times had it just been her and him, alone, in the room together?

Too many to count.

Dean continued, "So after he killed Clint, he went after Julie, knowing she had the code as well. She was on her way to see Trevor when Jesse lured her behind the woodpile, threatened her for the code and then shot her after she gave it to him. His plan was to get the money and leave town that night... he'd booked a one-way flight to Mexico. And by the way, we found a shrine of Eve in his cabin—he was obsessed with her."

She covered her heart with her hand, a feeble attempt to stop the racing. "But why try to kill me? I didn't know a damn thing about the money."

"Jesse assumed Clint had told you that he was going to meet him, the night he died. After Jesse killed him, he needed to tie up loose ends—you."

"I can't believe it, Dean." Her voice weakened. "I just can't believe it." She looked at him; his body was tense, his eyes reflecting a fire in his soul. Something else was going on. He wasn't telling her something.

"Dean?"

He tore his gaze away from the window.

"What else? You're not telling me something."

He began pacing.

She scooted to the edge of her seat. "Tell me, Dean."

He shook his head, clenched his fists.

"*Tell me.*"

He took a deep breath and his voice cracked as he said, "Jesse killed my dad. Seven years ago, Jesse killed my dad."

She surged to her feet. "*What?*"

She met him in front of the fireplace as he told her the story.

"Jesse was a young boy, sixteen at the time, and had been trespassing on our land for months. Of course, we didn't know it was him at the time. He'd carved on our trees, spray painted a shed, shot through the barn windows, opened the gates to let the cows out—things like that; tormenting us for fun, I guess. One day, one of our horses went missing and my dad had enough. A few days later, my dad saw someone in the woods, again—Jesse—and he sent a few warning shots into the air, to send him a message. A message to stay off his land." His hand trembled and he shoved them into his pockets. "The next night, my dad had gone to do a quick perimeter check and must've spotted Jesse in the woods. They got into an argument and Jesse shot him. Right between the eyes." He paused, his body tensing from head to toe. "After I found my dad's body, I shot fifteen rounds into the woods, praying that one of the bullets would hit the son of a bitch that had just killed my dad. When I arrested Jesse the other night, I noticed an old bullet wound on his shoulder, and I just knew. I knew in my gut, that second. Jesse killed my dad." He looked down and blew out a breath. "And Wesley, our ballistics expert, confirmed it with the bullet casing that I found that night—it matches Jesse's gun."

She closed the inches between them, wrapped her arms around him and began weeping.

And to her shock, so did he.

* * *

The fresh scent of spring flowers perfumed the air as Heidi stepped onto the porch.

"Thank you again, Mrs. Wilson."

"Of course. So I'll see you this Sunday for the open house."

"Sounds great."

As she watched the realtor walk to her sedan, she heard the rumble of a truck coming up the driveway. She smiled.

Dean waved at Mrs. Wilson as he rolled to a stop in front of the house.

He got out, with one hand tucked behind his back.

She cocked her head and met him at the bottom of the porch steps. "Whatcha got behind your back?"

He leaned down, kissed her forehead and handed her a bouquet of spring flowers. "Flowers for the most beautiful woman in the world."

She smiled. "They're so pretty. Thank you."

He smiled down at her. "How'd the meeting go?"

"Good, the open house is Sunday. I can't wait to sell this place."

In the months following the death of Clint and Julie, Earl's estate had entered probate, considering that the sole heirs to his fortune had passed away. The judge ruled the estate be split between the remaining spouses of Earl's children—Heidi and Julie's husband. Along with a significant amount of money and stocks, Heidi was given the Berry Springs Estate, while Julie's husband received the multiple vacation homes and a nice chunk of change for himself.

As of today, the estate was officially up for sale.

"You know, this place looks different in the spring. Happier, warmer, less *cold*." Heidi pushed through the front door with Dean right behind her.

"This is one of the nicest places in town, it's kind of legendary in Berry Springs. I'm sure you'll have no problem selling it."

They walked into the kitchen and Heidi grabbed a vase from the cupboard and began filling it with water. "I can't wait to get rid of it, honestly. Way too big."

Dean came up behind her, wrapping his arms around her waist. "If that's true, you sure as hell are going to love your new digs."

She smiled and looked down at her brand-new engagement ring at the exact moment it caught the light and sparkled across the sink. She turned and wrapped her arms around him. "I can't wait to move into your shoebox."

He smiled, kissed her lips. "I can't wait to marry you."

Her stomach tickled, her heart swelled and she laid her head on his warm, muscular chest—her safe place.

"I love you Dean, so much."

He squeezed her. "I love you too."

*If you enjoyed THE STORM, check out
the sneak peek below of the next book in
the series!*

THE FOG

BERRY SPRINGS
BOOK #4

A THICK CLOUD crept across the full moon as he turned left, up his driveway. Dark shadows from the surrounding woods danced across the dirt road that snaked up to his compound. Wesley glanced at the clock and blew out a breath—almost midnight.

It had been a hell of an evening, and an even worse date. *First* date. First and *last*.

She was nice enough, and attractive enough, but dammit, there was simply no chemistry between them.

Zero. Zip. Nada.

He had been bored to tears, which said a hell of a lot considering they met at his most favorite restaurant on the planet, Chub's BBQ. He'd even ordered the baby-backs—but no amount of fall-off-the-bone meat could've helped that date. He'd felt like he was on a date with his damn sister, which, by the way, was the one who set up the glorious meeting in the first place.

It's time to settle down and quit thinking of women as little toys, Wesley, she'd told him.

Maybe she was right, but it wasn't his fault if he didn't feel chemistry, right? Okay, so maybe he was picky—*extremely picky*—and maybe he wasn't ready to hang up his and her towels in the bathroom, but so what? What was wrong with that? He had his whole life to make the mind-boggling, life-long commitment of marriage.

Why rush?

And besides, if the last eight years of being a Marine had taught him anything, it was that life was short—too short.

He drove to the back of the main house and parked outside the door that led to the basement. Nothing helped ease the mind more than blaring some classic rock and getting his hands dirty in his gun shop. He turned off the engine, grabbed his cell phone, his Sig, and got out of his blacked-out Ford Platinum.

The moment his boot hit the dirt, the back of his neck tingled.

Something wasn't right.

He shoved his cell phone in his pocket—to free up a hand—and slid his finger over the trigger of his gun.

A light breeze swept over his skin as he briskly stepped across the driveway to the side of the house, under the cover of shadows.

He looked around.

The moonlight washed over the fields in the distance, disappearing into the dense woods of the Ozark Mountains.

No vehicles, no people, no lights, no sounds, nothing.

But something was wrong, he knew it in his gut.

He moved silently and fluidly along the side of the house, effortlessly fading into the background, as he had been trained to do.

He paused and glanced into the kitchen window—the house was dark inside, just the way he'd left it.

He came up on the basement door, his senses piqued.

Gun steady in his head, he reached for the knob.

Unlocked.

A fucking break-in.

Adrenaline—now mixed with anger—began to pulse through his body.

They picked the wrong fucking house to break into, he thought as he raised his gun.

A quick inhale to clear his head and like a flash of lightning, he burst through the door, gun raised.

Silence.

With his head on a swivel and finger on the trigger, he flicked the lights.

"Fucking son of a bitch."

His workshop was turned upside down, completely ransacked. Tools, equipment, parts, bullets, half assembled guns, all over the floor. He scanned the room—the house was still and dead silent.

With his gun raised, eyes and ears alert, he walked across the room to his walk-in gun safe, which held over fifty of his prized guns—half of which he'd made from scratch.

He exhaled loudly. The door was locked, the keypad that held his twenty-two-digit code still intact.

Thank God!

A breeze blew in from the opened door behind him, carrying with it a sweet, metallic scent.

His back straightened like a rod.

He knew that scent. Yes, he was very, very familiar with that scent.

He slowly turned, a chill running up his spine. He stealthily moved to the back wall and as he began to cross the massive room, the scent became stronger.

Oh, shit.

His pulse picked up, flashbacks of searching bombed buildings in Iraq raced through his head. The demolished buildings were rancid with the same scent—the smell of fresh blood.

Goosebumps broke out over his arms as he edged farther down the wall.

He rounded the corner, and stopped on a dime.

The silver light of the moon streamed in through a tiny window, illuminating a body, face down on the floor.

Fuck.

He lowered the gun, but kept his finger on the trigger, and walked over to the figure on the floor.

He looked down.

His blood ran ice-cold.

He knew that body. He knew that long, blonde hair.

He knew that bracelet.

At his feet, lay the motionless body of his ex-girlfriend, in a puddle of blood.

ABOUT THE AUTHOR

Amanda McKinney

Amanda McKinney, author of Sexy Murder Mysteries, wrote her debut novel, LETHAL LEGACY, after walking away from her career to become a writer and stay-at-home mom. Her books include the BERRY SPRINGS SERIES, and BLACK ROSE MYSTERY SERIES. Amanda lives in Arkansas where she is busy crafting her next murder mystery.

Visit her website at www.amandamckinneyauthor.com.

Made in the USA
Lexington, KY
25 July 2018